March Anson ar

of the U.

Marshall McClintock

Alpha Editions

This edition published in 2022

ISBN : 9789356786844

Design and Setting By
Alpha Editions
www.alphaedis.com
Email - info@alphaedis.com

Contents

CHAPTER ONE

FAREWELL TO THE *PLYMOUTH*

The launch purred smoothly across the calm waters of the harbor, making for the Navy Yard pier. Their feet braced against the slow roll of the boat, two young men stood looking at the huge gray ship they had just left.

"I'm beginning to have my doubts," Scoot Bailey said almost to himself.

"Same here," the other replied. March Anson was shorter than his friend, but more solidly and compactly built. His gray-blue eyes were steady and cool, matching the set of his jaw, but the crinkling lines at their corners showed that this apparently serious young man spent a good deal of time smiling or laughing.

"She was a swell ship," Scoot said sadly.

"*Was?*" exclaimed March. "She still is! Just because Bailey and Anson have left her, don't you think she can carry on any longer?" A slow smile spread over his face as he turned to look at his friend. But Scoot was serious.

"Oh, sure, March," he replied. "But she's out of our lives now. She's past tense for us. And—well, she's been just about everything to us for a year now—home, mother, and sweetheart!"

"I know what you mean," March said. "And it's natural for us to wonder if we've done the right thing in being transferred. Right now we're looking at what we're leaving. In another ten minutes we'll be concentrating on what we're going to!"

Scoot Bailey turned around and sat down.

"I'm going to start right now," he grinned. "No use getting sentimental about the old *Plymouth* at this point. I'm going to start thinking about the *Lexington* or the *Shangri-La* or whatever aircraft carrier I'll be on in a few months."

"Good idea," March agreed, sitting beside the tall and gangling young man who now stared ahead at the Navy Yard. "But that's one trouble right now, Scoot. Neither one of us knows exactly where he'll be. If you knew exactly what ship you'd be attached to, you could make your thoughts more specific. When you get there, you know you'll love her just as much as you've loved the *Plymouth*—more, in fact, because you'll be flying at last!"

"Yes, I know, but what about you?" Scoot asked. "I still can't figure out why you want to be a pigboat man. And what can you dream about now as you look into the future? The name of some fish, that's all."

"Sure, subs are named after fish," March replied. "And they have some swell names, too—the *Barracuda*, the *Dolphin*, the *Spearfish*, the *Amberjack*!"

"Yes, they sound all right," Scoot grinned. "But what if you're assigned to the *Cod* or the *Herring* or the *Shad*? No, I can't figure out what you see in those stuffy, cramped, oversized bathtubs!"

This light-hearted argument had been going on ever since March Anson and Scoot Bailey had been in the Navy together. Neither one minded the jibes of the other, but the dispute as to the respective merits of air and underwater craft never ended.

"Cozy and snug," March said stoutly, "that's what subs are! Not cramped and stuffy! Why—they're all air-conditioned now!"

"Maybe so," Scoot said, shaking his head, "but no air-conditioning can match the clear blue sky a couple of miles up there where I'll be flying! Boy—what a chance! Just what I've always wanted!"

Their departure from the cruiser *Plymouth* was forgotten now as they thought of their futures. Only one aspect of that future was rarely mentioned by either of them, and they tried not to think too much about it. In their new activities they would not be together—these two who had been inseparable friends for so many long years.

They had met in the first year of high school, back in that small Ohio city which now, during war, seemed so many miles and so many years away. Scoot had lived in Hampton all his life, but March had just moved there from the farm which his mother had sold when his father died. A widow with a son only thirteen years old could not run a 160-acre farm, she had decided, not if her son was to get the education she had determined he would have.

So the farm had been sold, and Mrs. Anson and her young son had moved to the near-by city of Hampton. March started high school, and his mother went back to teaching, her profession before she married Clement Anson and settled down to farm life. The money from the farm sale was tucked away in the bank, to be forgotten until the time came for March to enter college.

March and Scoot had sat next to each other in the big assembly hall of Hampton High School on the first day. They had taken to each other at once and from that time had been the closest of friends. Some people had wondered at the deep friendship of these two who, in some ways, seemed so different. Scoot had always been a noisy and boisterous kid, eager for any activity that meant speed, excitement, and a little bit of danger. The more conservative parents shook their heads and called him a little "wild" although he never got into serious trouble.

March Anson, on the other hand, was quiet and serious. On the farm he had worked hard and had learned the value of hard work. In school he studied thoroughly and carefully. Even in sports he was serious, playing games as though he looked on them as work, not as pleasure.

But March and Scoot recognized in each other at once the hidden qualities that lay beneath the surface indications of their character. Scoot saw that March really enjoyed life tremendously. He just didn't whoop and shout about it. He felt a thrill of pleasure in a tough football game played hard. He loved the talk and chatter of a gang of boys discussing the game afterward, even though he spent more time listening than talking himself. He liked the school dances, even though he was somewhat timid with girls and danced so quietly that he stood out in contrast to the majority of wildly capering youngsters.

Scoot learned to appreciate the slow smile that spread over March's face when he was enjoying himself. When something amusing happened, he could look at March and see the twinkle in his eye that others seemed to miss.

In the same way, March saw that beneath Scoot's noisy impulsiveness there was a great deal of calm courage, a daring that had in it nothing of foolhardiness but—on the contrary—a good deal of confidence. Scoot had a serious side that none of his friends, until March came along, had penetrated. He never seemed to study much, but his grades were always good. That was because Scoot never announced, "No, I can't do that—I have to go home and study now." Scoot was ready to do anything suggested by anyone, but he still managed to get his studying done, after the play was over.

By the time they graduated from high school together, Scoot and March had both changed a good deal, each one influenced by the other. At a first glance they seemed just the same as always, but March was less retiring, less timid, while Scoot did not always hide under his playful spirit his more serious interests in life.

When they went off to the state university together, they wondered how long it would last, for war was already in the air.

"It's coming," Scoot said, "just as sure as shootin', war's coming. And I'm going to be in it just about five minutes after it starts."

"They've been staving it off for a long time," March said, "and maybe they can keep it up a few years longer. But I don't think they can ever satisfy that Hitler guy. Giving in to a pig won't work—he'll just keep demanding more and more! But maybe we'll get our college education before the guns start popping!"

But the guns had started firing in Europe before their second year. When the first peacetime selective service act was passed in the United States, Scoot was very excited at being below the twenty-year age, and wanted to enlist at once. But it was March who persuaded him against it.

"We can do more good going right on getting our education until they need us," he insisted. "Then we'll be that much better equipped to do a good job."

His argument prevailed over Scoot then, but the war became their favorite topic of conversation from that time on. Many others in the college were not interested. They felt that the war was thousands of miles away, that two big oceans were enough insulation to keep it away from America.

But Scoot and March felt sure it was coming. They followed the war news carefully, their hearts sinking as Hitler's gangs overran one country after another in Europe. They spent their spare time reading books and articles about the war, the new weapons and tactics that were being used. It was then that Scoot knew that he wanted to be a flier, and then that March first developed his interest in submarines.

"This is an air war!" Scoot insisted. "It's going to be fought and won in the air!"

"The whole thing?" March demanded. "I wouldn't deny the importance of planes, but I'd never agree that they'll do the whole job alone. The country *without* planes can't win, I'll say that much. But look at Germany's U-boats! Look at the damage they're doing! If England can't get her supplies by sea— why, she's sunk!"

The argument that never ended was begun right then. March and Scoot read everything they could lay their hands on about submarines and airplanes. And when the Japs attacked Pearl Harbor, Scoot wanted to get in a plane and fly by instinct out over the Pacific, to give them a taste of their own medicine. He had just decided to enlist when the Navy's program for college students was announced—the V-12 plan which carried students through an intensive training course which resulted in commissions as Ensigns.

For March there was no doubt about what course to follow. He signed up for V-12 at once, already sure that he would be sailing in a submarine before the year was out.

Scoot could not make up his mind for a few days. When he had thought of flying, he had always thought of the Army Air Forces. But the Navy had fliers, too. Eventually it was his burning hatred of the Japs that decided him.

"There's a lot of water between us and them," he said. "The Navy will have the biggest job in knocking them over—and aircraft carriers will be the answer! Navy it is for me, too!"

So March Anson and Scoot Bailey had joined the Navy. Gone were all thoughts of football, baseball, dances, and parties. And suddenly there seemed to be little difference between the two. Both were now serious, hardworking, for in the Navy's program there was room for little but serious, hard work. Together they crammed into their heads more mathematics than they had thought of studying in a whole college course. Navigation, engineering, English, Navy custom and tradition—all were crammed into them with an intensity of which they had never thought themselves capable.

Both had put in early their requests for assignment to submarines and to air service. And, though they knew that the Navy tried to place men where they wanted to go, they realized that the Navy's needs would come first rather than their wishes. So they were disappointed, though not surprised, when both requests were turned down. The submarine school at New London, even though greatly expanded, was full to overflowing. And the applicants for Naval Aviation exceeded by ten times the number that could be accepted.

New warships were coming off the ways in shipyards all over the country, and men were needed to man them. So, after some further specialized training—Scoot in engineering and March in navigation—they found themselves assigned to the new cruiser *Plymouth* which had been rushed to completion four months ahead of schedule.

On their shakedown cruise they had been too interested in their new life—the huge ship and the men they worked with—to feel disappointment over missing out on their chosen fields. They knew they were already a part of the war, and the job they were doing was important. As Ensigns, they were two very junior officers on the ship almost as large as their home town, but they had their jobs, and they learned more about them and about all ships every day.

The Navy lost no time, after ship and crew were deemed fit and ready for action, in getting them to the Pacific where the losses suffered at Pearl Harbor had put the United States at a great, though temporary, disadvantage. By the time they had made the long trip down the eastern coast, through the Panama Canal, and across almost half the Pacific to Pearl Harbor, Scoot and March felt like veterans. The Executive Officer of the *Plymouth*, Commander Seaton, had taken a liking to them because of their application to their jobs and their desire to learn all they could. He saw to it that they got varied experiences, shifting to different jobs carried out by junior officers from time to time.

In company with a battleship, two light cruisers, and twelve destroyers, they left Pearl Harbor as a task force heading for action in the southwest Pacific. And action was not long in coming.

In the Coral Sea, the small task force ran into a Jap convoy, heavily screened by warships, trying to sneak an end run around the corner of Australia. Two U.S. aircraft carriers had gone out to break up the convoy, but they were so outnumbered by the enemy that they were in a bad way when the *Plymouth's* force arrived on the scene under full steam. The Japs were taken by surprise, lost their tight organization, and fled north, leaving behind three troopships and four destroyers heading for the bottom.

Scoot had been joyful at his first battle experience, but was angry that he had not been on the guns.

"Just when the fighting starts I have to be down in the engine room," he moaned. "Didn't even *see* anything, let alone take a shot at those dirty Nips!"

"Well, I *saw* plenty," March replied, "but navigation officers don't get a chance at much shooting, either!"

Scoot, by dint of much pleading and arguing, got Commander Seaton to transfer him to gunnery, but then eight weeks went by without a sight of a Jap. The first shots Scoot fired were into shore installations of the Japs at Munda airfield in the Solomons, after the Marines had consolidated their hold on Guadalcanal and had decided to move forward to another island.

The big battle had come almost ten months after they had shipped aboard the *Plymouth*, up in the Bismarck Sea northeast of New Guinea. Finally finding the sizable Jap force for which he had been looking, Admiral Caldwell, in charge of the U.S. force, had steamed right into the middle of the bevy of Jap ships and opened fire with everything he had. For seven hours, mostly at night, the battle had raged. Jap planes were attacking overhead, at least until U.S. planes drove them off at dawn. The firing on all sides was so deafening that no one could hear even Scoot's whoops of glee and happiness. When three of his gun crew went down under a hail of flying fragments from a shell that landed on the *Plymouth's* deck not fifty feet away, Scoot carried on with the few that were left, but the rate of fire was cut. So he rounded up a cook and a messboy and turned them into expert gunners in five minutes and knocked three Jap planes out of the sky with his improvised gun crew in ten minutes.

Meanwhile, March had not been idle. The shell whose fragments had laid low part of Scoot's crew had landed squarely on one of the 12-inch gun turrets forward. March was the first man into the smoking and wrecked turret, pulling out the wounded and dead who were there. At any moment the ammunition below might have exploded—for no one knew if the shell had penetrated that far—but March had no thought of such a thing. Three of the men he lugged from the turret were still alive, though closer to death than March had ever seen anyone. Later, the medical officer told March those three had lived only because they got medical attention so fast.

When it was all over, and half the Jap force lay at the bottom of the sea while the rest ran for cover, pursued by American planes, the men on the *Plymouth* wearily surveyed the damage done to their ship. It was plenty, but a month in port would fix her up again. As they headed slowly for Pearl Harbor for repairs, Scoot and March got the big surprise of their lives. They had no thought of making heroes of themselves, and they never could figure out how, in the heat of battle, any officer could have seen just what they did.

Yet when the citations came along, Scoot and March both found themselves on the list commended for conspicuous gallantry in action.

"My golly, we didn't do anything," Scoot had objected, even though he was beaming all over with pleasure. "Everybody else did the same kind of thing. All the crew were fighting just as hard as we were!"

"Yes, but they didn't all keep their heads under fire and show the spontaneously clear thinking that you two did," Commander Seaton said to them in a friendly talk later. "That's what counts—that's what makes leaders of men. And the Navy needs leaders these days. By the way, the Skipper asked me if there was anything special we could do for you two—anything you wanted especially. I told him that you, Scoot, had wanted to be a Navy flier and that March had wanted to be a submariner. If you still feel that way, the Skipper'll recommend your transfer to those branches."

March and Scoot were dumbfounded! And it had not been an easy thing to decide, though a few months before they would not have hesitated for an instant. Scoot still wanted to fly. March still wanted to go into the pigboats. But they had lived on the *Plymouth*, gone through battle with her, and they didn't like the idea of leaving her now.

It was March who made up his mind first. "I'm going to ask for the transfer," he said. "I hate to leave this ship and the men on it and the action I know she'll be seeing. After a battle or two you don't feel like going back to school again. You want to go on to more battles. But I love the idea of submarines so much that I know I'd be a better man in a pigboat than I can ever be on a surface ship. So I'll take a few months out, learn what I have to learn, and come back to this part of the world and really send some of those Jap ships to the bottom."

"Guess you're right," Scoot agreed. "It won't be long!"

So they had said farewell to the *Plymouth* sadly as they stepped into the launch taking them ashore. And they had stood looking at the great gray ship as the little boat moved toward the Navy Yard pier.

But now their eyes were set forward. They had a long way to travel to get home, a lot of hard work and studying to do before they could accomplish what they wanted.

They stepped from the launch and stood on the pier. For a last moment they looked out at the *Plymouth* once more.

"So long, old gal," Scoot said. "You'll be getting your face lifted here at Pearl Harbor and you'll be back in the thick of it soon. Maybe I'll see you out there—when I'm up in the blue sky flying my Grumman Wildcat."

"Yes, and some time when I'm submerged and hear the throb of a cruiser's engines," March added, "I'll stick up the periscope for a peek, wondering whether that ship is friend or foe. And it'll turn out to be my old friend, my old sweetheart, the *Plymouth*."

Together, the two young men turned and walked toward their new lives.

CHAPTER TWO

BACK TO SCHOOL

March felt lonely as he stood on the corner opposite the railroad station in New London, waiting for the bus. It was cold and there was rain in the air. The wind whipped about him as he stood close to the building.

The *Plymouth* was a world miles away by this time, although it had been less than a month since he left it. First there had been the wait of a few days in Hawaii before they found space in a plane heading back for the United States. But those had been good days—interesting in that they saw how completely erased were the effects of the first terrible Jap attack. Then, too, there had been time to rest, to swim and to lie in the sun on the beach.

Finally the long over-water hop had brought them back to America, which they had left so long before. It was the first time either March or Scoot had been in San Francisco, and they enjoyed the two days spent there before taking the train east. Finally there had been two weeks' leave back in Hampton. They had seen their parents, visited their old friends, slept late and eaten huge meals. They had even been persuaded to make an embarrassed appearance—supposed to be accompanied by speeches—in the assembly hall of the old high school.

Their leave had come to an end all too soon. Then both young men had been faced with the prospect of saying goodbye not only to their folks and their friends, but to each other. It was one fact that both of them had tried to avoid thinking about, but as the time approached they were very aware of it. For so many years they had been together almost every day—but they had taken each other for granted. It never occurred to them that they were closer than many brothers, that each one supplied something necessary and important to the other.

They couldn't say much, of course, when they finally did say goodbye. It was March's train which left first, although Scoot would be heading south only two hours later. They were all at the station in Hampton—March's mother, Scoot's father and mother and kid sister. March had to say goodbye to all of them and step on to the train alone.

He shook hands with Scoot. "My golly," he stammered, "I'm going to be worried about you, Scoot. You've had me around to look after you and keep you out of trouble so long, that I don't know how you'll make out alone."

They all laughed a little, and Scoot tried to kid back at March, but his heart wasn't in it.

"Don't worry about me," he replied. "I think the baby is busy worrying about the nurse this time. Anyway, if it makes you feel good, March, maybe you'll have a chance to get me out of trouble later—out in the Pacific somewhere."

"Say—maybe I will at that!" March tried to act serious. "I can just see myself dashing up in my trusty submarine and rescuing you from a bunch of Japs."

Later, when they *did* meet under circumstances not very different from March's joking suggestion, it was Scoot who remembered what his friend had said back in the station in Hampton, Ohio.

But at the time it was nothing but banter, the kind of talk made to cover up real thoughts that are too deep to be expressed easily. And in another moment the train came thundering down the track. There was a last hurried round of goodbyes and March was on the train, waving and smiling from the car platform as it pulled away from his home.

Because the train was crowded, March had been busy trying to find a place to sit. His suitcase on the same platform was the seat he finally chose, until they pulled into Pittsburgh and he found a more comfortable seat.

The ride had been dirty and uninteresting and March felt himself getting depressed long before they reached New York. There he had to rush to get the train for New London, and now he stood on that windy, rainy corner waiting for a bus, feeling sorry that he had ever won the chance to get into submarine work.

Then he remembered the one thing that had made him feel good since he had left Hampton, and he glanced down at the cuff of his sleeve. Yes—there it was—the extra stripe that had been added when he became a Lieutenant instead of the lowest of commissioned officers, an Ensign.

The promotion had come to them when they were in Hampton on leave—for both Scoot and March. They had quickly added the new stripes to cuffs, to shoulder boards, and had got the gold bars to wear on their work uniform shirts. March felt very proud and pleased, for the promotion had come quickly for such young men in the Navy. Going to the submarine school as a Lieutenant, even if only j.g., or junior grade, was much better than walking in as an Ensign.

He was staring at the stripes on his cuff and smiling so that he didn't notice the salute of the three men who approached him. Only when the first man spoke did he look up.

"Going to the sub base, sir?"

March saw a sailor with the insigne of a petty officer, third class, on his sleeve, a sturdy, smiling young man with his seabag over his shoulder. Behind him appeared three more men of the same rank. The first, March noticed, was a radioman, two of the others fire controlmen, and the last a pharmacist.

"Yes, waiting for the bus," March answered with a smile. "Is this the place to wait for it?"

"That's what we were told, sir," the radioman said. "You see, we're just reporting there for the school."

"Oh, so am I," March said. "I thought maybe you men were there already and just in town on liberty. But you wouldn't have brought your seabags along in such a case, would you?"

In a moment the bus appeared and they all climbed aboard. On the long ride out of town and along the river they talked together about the school they were going to, and March caught again, in these men's enthusiasm, his old feeling of excitement about going into submarines. The men, who had obviously just met as they went to the bus together, were discussing their reasons for volunteering for submarine duty.

"I had two uncles in the Navy," the pharmacist said. "I'll never forget the way they talked about submariners. They had both tried, but couldn't pass the tests. They thought the pigboat men were the cream of the fleet."

"Speaking of the hard tests," one of the fire controlmen said, "that's really why I first got the notion of applying for sub duty. I heard it was the toughest branch of the service to get into and stay in—and I just kind of like to try any challenge like that. When I hear about something really tough, I like to take a crack at it. This is harder to get into than aviation!"

"Going to the Sub Base, Sir?"

March smiled and thought of Scoot who had been worrying about his ability to meet the strict qualifications for naval fliers.

"I like the life on a sub," the radioman said. "You know—a good bunch of guys doin' something big together, all workin' together like a team. And the—well, friendliness between officers and men is swell. Not that I don't believe in strict discipline—" he glanced at the officer's stripes on March's cuff—"but I still think it's a good idea for officers and men to get friendly, get to know each other well, the way they do on subs."

March agreed, and noticed that not one of the men had mentioned the extra pay for submarine duty as one of the reasons for entering that branch, and a dangerous branch, of the naval service.

"That's a good sign," he told himself. "Of course, they'll like the extra pay—no doubt of that—but it's not the reason they volunteered for sub duty. They really go into it for its own sake."

The bus turned and entered the driveway of the sub base grounds and all the men looked eagerly out the windows. Their first look was for the river, where they hoped to see submarines.

"Look!" cried Scott, the radioman. "There's one in dry dock!"

"And over there by the pier," called another, "there's a bunch of 'em lined up."

March looked at the long slim lines of the pigboats and felt warm inside. He wondered just how soon he would take his first ride beneath the waters of Long Island Sound in one of them.

The bus passed a few buildings, but the sailors had no eyes for such ordinary things. Another structure had caught them—a tall round tower looming up above the trees on the gently sloping hillside.

"What's that?" one of the men asked. "A water tower?"

"Water tower's right!" exclaimed Scott. "But a special kind. That's the escape tower!"

"Oh-oh, that's the baby I'm wondering about," said the pharmacist. "I don't know how I'll like going up through a hundred feet of water with just a funny gadget clamped over my nose and mouth."

"Well—you better not let it get you," one of the others put in. "It's one of the first tests, I hear. If you can't handle the escape-tower tests, you're tossed out of submarines pronto!"

The bus pulled up in front of a large brick building and stopped. Everyone got out and walked up to the front door. Inside, March left the men with a smile and reported to the personnel man in charge of receiving new officers assigned to the school. In another half hour he found himself in his quarters in a building some way up the hill above the main buildings of the base. Here the school itself was situated, with its buildings for classrooms, barracks for enlisted men, and quarters for officers without wives. Married officers were allowed to live in New London with their families and commute daily to the school.

March's room was small but comfortable, and he was neatly settled in it in a short while. His time in the Navy had taught him already to travel light, with only the necessary belongings, and to settle himself quickly. He was at home and comfortable by the time he reported to the officers' mess for dinner.

There he met other young officers who also lived at the school, and a few of the instructors. The latter were older men, full of years and wisdom in the submarine service, every one of whom would much rather have been on active duty hunting down Jap or Nazi ships on the oceans of the world. But they were too valuable in the great task of training the hundreds of new officers needed for the subs coming off the ways of the shipyards. Here in New London they could pass on to the younger men like March Anson a portion of their knowledge of pigboats.

March felt, during dinner, the quiet good-fellowship of these men. On the *Plymouth* the officers with whom he ate and talked and played were pleasant and agreeable fellows, but there had been all types there—the quiet ones, the back-slappers, the life-of-the-party men with practical jokes and loud guffaws, the grimly serious officers, and everything in between. But here the men were more alike.

"Not that they're all the same," he told himself, as he looked around the table. "McIntosh here next to me is quite different in most ways from that Lieutenant Curtin across the table, for instance, but they have something in common. Something similar in their personalities, I suppose. They're sociable, but in a quiet way. They're serious, but not without a sense of humor."

March did not realize that he was describing himself when he thought of the other officers in this way. But he might have known that this question of personality was one of the most important in considering men who volunteered for submarine service.

No man in the Navy was ever assigned to sub work without his request. It was an entirely volunteer service, but there were always far more applications, among both officers and enlisted men, than could be accepted. So it was possible for the Bureau of Navy Personnel to keep its standards very high in selecting men for the pigboat branch.

When a man already in the Navy was recommended by his commanding officer for assignment to the sub school at New London, as March had been, this did not mean that the recommendation was accepted just like that. The Bureau looked over the man's record with the greatest care. And just bravery such as March had displayed was not enough, even though it counted strongly in his favor. What they looked for in the "Diving Navy" was the kind of man who was brave, cool under fire, far above the average intelligence, with the ability to get along well with other people under all circumstances, and the kind of nerves that didn't crack or even show strain under the greatest danger, the worst crowding, or seemingly fatal situations.

As March thought of this, he swelled with pride to think he had been chosen for the submarine school.

"But that's just the beginning," he told himself. "I feel pretty darned good to know that I've got this far, but they're going to watch me like a hawk every moment I'm here. I think I can pass all the tough physical tests okay, because I'm in good shape. The studies are hard but if I work enough maybe I can handle them. But how will I act the first time I'm in a submerging sub? How will I react to a crash dive? They'll be watching me. And even if I get through the school I'm still not a submariner. Why, on my first real trip or two my commanding officer can transfer me back to surface ships just by saying the word!"

After dinner, in the officers' lounge, March spoke with the executive officer of the sub base, a kindly, gray-haired man with skin that still looked as if he spent a few hours every day facing the salt breeze on a ship's bridge. Captain Sampson chatted easily with March as they looked out the windows at the gathering twilight.

"Glad to have you with us, Anson," he said. "Hope you like it here."

"I'm sure I will, sir," March replied. "I've been looking forward to it long enough."

"I had an idea this was no sudden impulse of yours," Sampson replied. "First off, you're not the kind, I take it, that acts on sudden impulses. And I imagine that subs always appealed to you."

"Yes, before I was in the Navy that's what I wanted."

"Then you ought to do very well," the Captain said. "You'll want to make your call on the Commandant tomorrow, I suppose?"

"If it can be arranged," March said.

"Yes—tomorrow will be all right, I'm sure," Sampson said, "for you to present your compliments to him. There'll be a few more officers arriving for the new class tomorrow morning early. I've set aside a couple of hours in the afternoon for the calls. Report at fifteen o'clock."

"Yes, sir," March said.

When the Captain had gone, March went back to his quarters and sat down to write a few letters. The first was to Scoot Bailey.

"Dear Scoot," it began. "I'm here at last—at the Submarine School in New London! Tomorrow things will really start!"

CHAPTER THREE

FIFTY POUNDS OF PRESSURE

Things really did start the next day for March! In the morning he had a physical examination that made all his previous examinations look like quick once-overs. Eyes, ears, lungs, heart, stomach—they went over March's body so thoroughly that he felt not a microbe, not a blood cell, had escaped their detection. But he knew, without waiting for the report, that he had no difficulty in meeting all the requirements.

In the afternoon there was the official call on the Commandant, which was not the stiff and formal ceremony such Naval customs often are, but an interesting and heart-warming experience. The "Old Man" really took the time to talk informally and in very friendly fashion with the new officers who came to the school.

March met the new officers who were just beginning their work at the school with him, got his schedule of duties for the next few days, and managed to work in a letter to his mother in the evening.

The next day, when March learned that he had passed his physical examination with flying colors, he also learned that one of the doctors examining him had been a psychiatrist.

"That's the smartest thing yet!" he muttered to Ensign Bigelow, another new officer-student who had just come from a teaching assignment at one of the Navy's technical schools. "Usually the psychological examination is separate. You know you're going to be questioned by a psychiatrist who will ask you all sorts of strange questions about how you get along with girls and what you thought of your fifth-grade teacher, and—"

"And what your dreams are like," added Bigelow.

"Sure, and you're self conscious," March went on. "A smart doctor probably sees through that and gets the real dope as to what makes your personality tick, but it has always struck me as a sort of silly business."

"Same here," Bigelow agreed. "Even though I know those Navy psychiatrists have been right about ninety-nine percent of the time."

"But this was wonderful!" March exclaimed. "I just thought those three docs were all looking at blood pressure and listening to my heart and such things. Sure, one of them was especially friendly and talked to me a lot, but that was just natural. And, come to think of it, he talked a lot about what I did when I was on the *Plymouth*, and how I liked its Skipper, and where I'd gone to school."

"I remember now," Bigelow said, "that he asked me about my leave before I came here. Mentioned big drinking parties. I didn't go in for any and said so. I thought he must be a heavy drinker from the way he talked, but he was just finding out whether *I* was or not."

"He pulled the same line on me," March said, "and I just thought it was making talk—you know, the way a dentist does before he does something that hurts, to take your mind off what's happening."

"Well, that won't be the end of the psychological tests," Bigelow said. "I understand that a psychiatrist is always there when we make our first dives, and he's just happening to be around in the escape-tower tests. He's keeping an eye on us all the time."

"Some people might not like that idea," March said. "I suppose they wouldn't like the idea of having somebody looking them over to spot their bad reactions to everything that goes on."

"Like a guilty conscience," Bigelow added.

"Always on hand," March grinned. "But I don't think it's a bad idea. After all, it's for our own protection. They've got to try to weed out the guys who will crack at the wrong time. And nobody thinks he will, so you can't find it out just by asking. If I'm that kind, then you don't want to find yourself out in the Pacific undergoing a depth-charge attack with me alongside you, suddenly going nuts inside a very small submarine."

"I should say not," Bigelow said. "And it's nothing especially against a fellow if he can't stand this particular kind of strain that he gets in a sub. Maybe he's got a kind of claustrophobia—fear of being shut up in small places—without knowing it. Maybe he'd make a swell aviator or bombardier or the bravest PT-boat Skipper in the world! It's just that submarining takes certain qualities, that's all. You've either got 'em or you haven't."

"And those docs find it out before you go out," March agreed.

March spent the evening with Bigelow and began to like the red-headed young man more as he got to know him better. Stan Bigelow was a chunky, broad-shouldered fellow who looked so hard that a tank could not bowl him over. A broken nose, covered with freckles, added greatly to his appearance of toughness, even though it had come, as he told March, from nothing more pugilistic than a fall out of a tree when he was sixteen years old.

"Landed just wrong on a pile of rocks," he said. "Didn't hurt a thing but my nose. I was at a summer camp and the doc there didn't fix it up right. By the time somebody tried to put it back into a decent shape the bones had set too well."

Despite Stan's look of a waterfront bruiser, he was really a serious-minded student. He had graduated from one of the country's top-flight engineering schools just before going into the Navy, and then had attended one of the Navy's technical schools. Diesel engines were his specialty and he felt sure that this knowledge would quickly get him into submarine work where he wanted to be. But his work at the technical school had been so brilliant that they kept him on as an instructor despite his pleas for transfer to New London. Finally, after a year of teaching, he had been recommended for submarines by an understanding commanding officer.

"So here I am," he concluded. "And right now I'm scared to death that it won't make any difference how much I want to be a submariner or how much I know about Diesels. If I get jittery in the pressure tank tomorrow—out I'll go!"

"You don't even need to get jittery," March laughed. "How do you know whether you can stand pressure or not? Even in perfect physical shape, some people just can't, that's all. I don't mean because they're nervous. Maybe their noses bleed or their ears won't make the right adjustment or something."

"Well—we won't know until we try it!" Stan exclaimed. "I'm just going to keep my fingers crossed."

After breakfast the next morning March and Stan Bigelow, along with the other new officer-students, reported to the little building at the base of the tall escape tower. They were joined by the new class of enlisted men who were to undergo the same tests. During preliminary training, there was no difference between officers and men in the examinations and work they had to undergo. Only later, when actual classes of study began, did they separate—for the enlisted men to learn their particular trades in reference to submarines and for the officers to get the highly technical studies and executive training they must have.

March saw Scott, the radio petty officer, and the others who had ridden to the sub base on the same bus with him. He called a friendly hello to them as they all stood waiting for the Chief Petty Officer in charge to call the roll.

After roll was called all the students were instructed to strip to the swimming trunks they had been instructed to wear, eyeing the pressure chamber suspiciously all the time.

"Looks like something to shut somebody up in if you never wanted him to get out," Stan Bigelow said, nodding at the huge gray-painted cylinder with its tiny portholes and small hatch-like door.

"Anyway, we can look out," March said, "even if the portholes are tiny."

"I wonder if that psychiatrist will be peeking in one of those deadlights at us," Stan mused, "making notes about every flicker of an eyelash."

But then the grizzled old Chief Petty Officer opened the small door to the chamber and ordered the new men inside. Stooping as he stepped in, March saw that the sides of the chamber had long benches, about twenty feet long, on which the men were to sit. The compartment was brightly lighted, and March noticed a fan in one corner.

"I guess it gets a little warm," he told himself, "with so many people in a small closed space like this."

Stan Bigelow sat beside him on the bench, and the other students filed in after them. March saw that Scott, the radioman, sitting opposite him, looked a little frightened, and he wondered if he appeared the same to the others.

"Funny how this gets you," Stan said in a low voice. "There's not a thing to be afraid of, of course."

"No, the most that can happen is that your nose will bleed or some small thing like that will show you can't stand pressure," March agreed. "But some of the older guys around here have had a lot of fun, particularly with the enlisted men, building up some fancy pictures of what the pressure tank and escape tower are like. They say you get weird sensations in your head, feel flutters in your heart."

"Oh—just a little bit of subtle freshman hazing," Stan laughed. "Well, I think the reason I'm nervous is that I don't want anything to happen to toss me out of submarines."

They looked toward the door of the compartment as the Chief Petty Officer stepped inside and tossed a bunch of robes on the seat near the door.

They Filed into the Pressure Chamber

"Wonder why the robes?" March muttered. "If anything, it's going to be too hot in here—that's why there's a fan."

"Maybe this is a combination test," Stan said with a grin. "They want to see if we can stand pressure—and heat."

The CPO closed and fastened securely the door, and they all heard someone on the outside testing it to be certain it was tightly shut.

"You're goin' to be out of here pretty fast," the officer said to the students, "so don't fret. We get fifty pounds of pressure in here, that's all."

His tone was casual and reassuring, but none of the men sat back in relaxed positions, even though they tried to appear completely at ease and even unconcerned. They almost jumped when the CPO banged his fist lustily against the end of the chamber as a signal to the man handling the valves outside.

They jumped again as a hissing sound filled the small compartment. The air was pouring in, and the men sat listening to it in silence. March saw that the Chief had his eyes on a dial at the end of the chamber and he looked there, too. Stan noted the direction of his glance, and in another moment every student was staring at the hand that moved up slowly to indicate one pound of pressure, then two pounds, then three pounds....

The CPO banged on the side of the chamber again. The hissing stopped. Everyone looked up in surprise, wondering if there was something wrong. March glanced around quickly. Was one of the students too jittery? Had a nosebleed started already? But everyone looked all right, except for an expression of worry.

"There's only three pounds pressure now," the Chief said. "Even fifty's not really a lot, but three's almost nothing. Still, just to give you an idea that air pressure is real pressure and not just something like a billowy cloud, I thought I'd tell you that we couldn't possibly open that hatch now. You see— when I say three pounds of pressure, that means per square inch. There's about a ton and a half of pressure on that door right now. Figure out how much there is on *you*."

With another bang the hissing of the inrushing air began once more and the hand on the dial began to creep around again, passing the figure five, then the figure ten, then fifteen. March began to feel uncomfortably warm, and then he saw that most of the other men were beginning to sweat. Stan leaned over and put his lips close to March's ear so that he could be heard over the sound of the air.

"Air under pressure gets hot," Stan said. "Remember your physics? It's the whole basis of a Diesel engine, incidentally, but the pressure is considerably greater. The temperature in a cylinder gets up to about a thousand degrees."

"Around a hundred in here now, I'd say," March replied in a loud whisper, and Stan nodded in agreement. Then he swallowed with some difficulty, and smiled in some surprise afterward.

"My ears popped when I swallowed;" he said. "Feels better."

"That's right," boomed the CPO, who had apparently noticed what Stan did. "Everybody try swallowing a few times if your ears feel funny."

March swallowed and then almost laughed as he saw the two rows of students earnestly swallowing. Then he realized he had not looked at the pressure dial for some time. He was startled to see it at thirty-five pounds. It was a good deal hotter now and everyone was sweating profusely. March looked around at the others carefully, forgetting his concern about himself in his interest in the others.

There seemed to be less tension now than at the very beginning. A few of the men talked to each other, comparing their reactions, laughing at the way their ears popped, expressing surprise at the increasing heat. Suddenly there was another banging on the wall of the chamber, and the hissing stopped. Everyone's eyes went to the pressure dial, and saw the hand standing at fifty pounds.

So this was it! Well, it wasn't so bad. March felt that way himself and saw the same feeling spreading to all the others, who smiled slightly as they knew they had withstood the pressure test successfully.

"So far, anyway," March told himself. "Some things happen occasionally, I guess, when the pressure is reduced."

Already the hand on the dial was moving downward again, as the air was released from the chamber by a man handling the valves on the outside. March began to feel cooler, and in a few minutes he shivered suddenly.

"Better put on the robes," the Chief said, tossing the robes to the men on the benches. "The temperature was up to a hundred and thirty for a while there, and it drops just as fast as the pressure drops."

"Feels good!" Stan said, as he slipped into the robe.

"Sure, but I'd like a couple of blankets, too," March replied, feeling his teeth begin to chatter.

They heard another pound on the wall and saw that the dial hand stood at ten pounds of pressure inside.

"We've got to stop it here for a while," the CPO explained. "There's a regular rate at which a man's got to come out of pressure to keep from getting the bends. You probably know something about the bends—every sailor does—but here's the idea. Your blood's under pressure in the arteries and veins, too, just like the rest of you, and there's oxygen and other things carried in that blood. When pressure is reduced too much too suddenly, some of the gases in your blood form bubbles—just like a kettle boiling. And those bubbles in your blood can cause plenty of trouble."

Stan turned to March. "Sure," he said. "Remember those experiments everybody has in first-year chemistry? Making water boil when you put it on a cake of ice? The water's under pressure in a closed container, and cooling it condenses the steam vapor so that pressure is reduced. So the air forms bubbles which escape when pressure goes down."

"I remember," March said. "They've got the bends licked now, though, since they know just how fast to reduce pressure."

More air was let out until the dial showed five pounds of pressure for a while, and then it was reduced to zero. The door was swung open by the Chief and the men stepped out of the chamber with smiles on their faces.

"One test passed," March said. "What's next?"

"The escape tower," Stan replied. "Tomorrow."

CHAPTER FOUR

UNDERWATER ESCAPE

When March returned to his quarters that afternoon he found a letter from Scoot Bailey waiting for him. It was full of excitement and enthusiasm, and it filled March with a good deal of envy.

"I've flown already!" Scoot wrote. "I didn't think we'd get around to it for quite a while, but I got up the third day I was here. Of course, I didn't handle the plane, really, but I just held my hand lightly on the stick while the instructor took me through a few simple turns and climbs. Just to give me the feel of it, he said, and so I'd know I really came here to fly, not just to study in classes."

March shook his head. "And to think that I've hardly seen a submarine!" he muttered to himself. "And I surely haven't been inside one. But Scoot's already been up in a plane! It just goes to show," he told himself, "that submarines are tougher than planes. Just think of the tests we've got to go through before they can even let us take a ride in a sub. With a flier all he's got to do is pass a physical test!"

"And speaking of classes," Scoot's letter went on, "they are really tough! Remember back in college we used to think we had to study fairly hard? Boy, we just had a picnic in those days! We'd look on that kind of business as a hilarious vacation down here."

March felt worse than ever. "I'm just wasting time!" he complained to himself. "Not even a class yet, and Scoot's studying already!"

He finished Scoot's letter quickly, learning that he had made a few good friends already, that he felt fine, that he loved flying. Then March sat down and wrote Scoot a long letter.

"I'll tell him about the pressure chamber," March said. "I'll show the lad that we're doing plenty here that he never even dreamed of. And I'll tell him about the escape tower we're going to have a try at tomorrow. That ought to show him that he's picked just an easy branch of the service."

So March wrote, and he told Scoot plenty. He made the test in the pressure chamber sound much more harrowing than it had actually been, even inventing one man who passed out, bleeding profusely, in the middle of the test.

Then he felt better, and went down to dinner feeling once more that he was in the cream of the Navy. As he walked down the hill he heard the drone of an airplane motor overhead.

"Simple," he said to himself. "See how easy it is? Just push a stick this way or that, just push a couple of pedals, and keep your eyes on a couple of dozen instruments. Why, in a sub we've got more instruments and dials than in twenty-five bombing planes!"

When he sat down next to Stan Bigelow, it was even better, for Stan agreed with him completely about the super-importance of the submarine service, thinking up a few additional reasons for its superiority over Naval Aviation that had not occurred to March. Then they began discussing the escape tower test the next day.

"Do you know much about this Momsen Lung they use?" Stan asked. "I saw some today when we took the pressure test, but I don't know the details of how they work."

"Yes, I read all about them a few years ago," March answered. "They were invented by an Annapolis man—then Lieutenant Charles Momsen—not much more than ten years ago. And you know, Stan, that guy conducted every single experiment himself—wouldn't let anybody else take the chance."

"Boy, he should have got a medal for that!" Stan exclaimed.

"He did! Distinguished Service Medal," March said. "And the Lung is one of the biggest things ever invented to make subs safer. Simple—really, like most good things. The good thing about it is that there's no connection at all with the outside. Most such devices had a valve system for letting the exhaled air out into the water. But the valves jammed shut—or open—too often. There's nothing like that to go wrong in the Momsen Lung."

"How does it get rid of the carbon dioxide that you breathe out?" Stan asked.

"There's a can of CO_2 absorbent inside it, that's all," March explained. "Of course, in time it wouldn't absorb any more, but how long are you ever going to use a Momsen Lung at one stretch, anyway?"

"Ten or fifteen minutes, I suppose," Stan replied.

"Sure," March agreed. "And the can of absorbent can take care of your carbon dioxide for a lot longer than that. And the rest of it is really just as simple. It's an airtight bag that straps over your chest. There's a mouthpiece you clamp between your teeth for breath, and a nose clip to close your nose so you won't breathe through it. When the bag's filled with oxygen—there you are!"

"Wonderful!" Stan said. "But doesn't that bag of oxygen, plus your own tendency to float, send you shooting up to the surface in a hurry?"

"It would if you let it," March replied. "That's why there always has to be a line or cable up to the surface, so you can hold on to it and keep yourself from ascending too quickly."

"And get the bends," Stan concluded. "If anything, I know I'll go more slowly than they tell me."

The next morning they had a chance to look more closely at the Momsen Lungs before they put them on, with the instructor explaining their workings and showing the students how to adjust them. March did not see Scott, the radioman, among the group, although all the others were the same that had gone through the pressure test the day before. He spoke to the young pharmacist, asking about Scott.

"Got a cold," was the reply. "Just a little nose cold, but they wouldn't let him do the escape test with it."

"Too bad," March said. "But he'll be able to catch up with the rest of us soon."

The Chief Petty Officer in charge was explaining the test to the men, as they got into their swimming trunks.

"First we'll have twenty pounds of pressure in the chamber," he said, "just to be sure noses and ears are in good shape before going into the water. And then you've got a long climb ahead of you. You see, the bottom of this tower is a hundred feet from the surface at the top. You won't be taking the hundred-foot escape for quite a while yet. Today we go up to the eighteen-foot level."

March thought that ought to be simple. He had been almost that far beneath the water sometimes when he went in swimming. But then he remembered that this test was to teach the men the proper use of the Momsen Lung, the rate of climb up the cable to the surface. It wasn't the pressure at eighteen feet that would bother anyone, unless it was somebody who had some deep fear of being under water.

"Such a person wouldn't very well select the submarine service, though," he said to himself. "Of course some people have these fears without knowing it. Nothing has ever happened to bring it out, that's all."

The time in the pressure chamber seemed like nothing after their fifty-pound session of the day before, and soon the students found themselves ascending to the eighteen-foot level of the tower.

"Up at the top," the Chief was saying, "there are plenty of men ready to take care of you. Nothing much is likely to go wrong with such a short escape, but we don't leave anything to chance. So if you get tangled in the cable or decide to go down instead of up, or anything like that, there's a few mighty good swimmers to do the rescue act. There's one thing to remember—we send you men up one after the other, pretty fast, just the way you'd be doin' it if you were getting out of a sub lyin' on the bottom of the ocean. So get away from the cable buoy fast, and without kickin' your legs all over the place. You're likely to kick the next one in the head, especially if he has come up a little too fast."

"How fast are we supposed to go, Chief?" one of the men asked.

"About a foot per second," the officer replied. "You hold yourself parallel with the cable, body away from it a little bit, and let yourself up hand over hand. You can put your hands about a foot above each other, and count off the seconds to yourself. We'll be timing you at both ends, so you'll find out afterwards whether you went too fast or too slow. Then you'll catch on to the rate all right."

March was among the first men who stepped into the bell at the eighteen-foot level. The water of the tower came up to his hips and was kept from going higher in the little compartment by the pressure of the air forced into the top of the bell-shaped room. He saw a round metal pipe shaped like a very large chimney extending down into the water.

"That skirt goes down a little below the water level in here on the platform," the Chief said. "When you go up, you fasten on your Lung, duck under the skirt, and go straight up. First, I'm going to check to be sure that the cable's set okay."

March and the others watched closely as the Chief adjusted his nose clips and mouthpiece deftly, turned the valve opening the oxygen into the mouthpiece, and ducked under. In a moment he reappeared and removed the Lung.

"All set," he said. "Okay, you—" he pointed to the young pharmacist, "you go first. Your Lung's filled with oxygen, plenty of it. There's the carbon dioxide absorbent in there to take up everything you breathe out. Remember to go up hand over hand, about a foot per second. And don't be surprised if a couple of guys go floatin' past you in the water on your way up. There're other instructors swimmin' around up there and once in a while one of 'em swims down to see how you're makin' out. All set?"

"Yes, Chief," the pharmacist answered. March thought he looked completely calm, though he felt himself growing excited at even this short escape.

"Okay, mouthpiece in place," the Chief said, making sure that the student did it correctly. "Now, nose clips on—that's right. Finally, open the valve so you can get the oxygen. Okay?"

The pharmacist nodded that he was all right. "On your way, then, my lad," the Chief said. "Duck under."

March watched the young man duck under the water and disappear as he went under the metal skirt. Then he saw the Chief go under, too, right behind him. Up above, he knew, the instructors would see a tug on the yellow buoy fastened to the cable, and would begin their timing of the first ascent. One of them would dive down and have a look at the student coming up, would make him pull away if he were hugging the cable too closely, speed him up or slow him down if necessary, with a gesture and a pat on the shoulder.

Suddenly the Chief reappeared.

Hand Over Hand He Ascended

"Okay, you," he said, pointing to March. As he put the mouthpiece in place, he thought how strange it was that in the tower in a pair of swimming trunks he was just plain "you" to the Chief Petty Officer, while in uniform outside he would be "sir."

"Right now," March thought as he adjusted the nose clips and turned the valve, "this man's my superior and my teacher. A young officer can learn plenty from these boys who've had so much experience, if they give themselves a chance by forgetting for a few minutes that they're commissioned officers."

As the Chief patted his shoulder, March ducked under the water, found the bottom of the round metal skirt, and went under it. Looking up, he saw the long shaft of darkness made by the walls of the tower, and the filmy, cloudy circle of half-light at the surface which suddenly seemed a great distance away. His hands had already found the cable, and he held on to it as he felt the upward tug of the Lung which tried to carry him swiftly to the top.

Putting one hand about a foot above the other he began to count to himself, hoping that his counts were about a second apart. For every count he put his hand up what he judged to be another foot in distance. Then he realized that his legs were unconsciously starting to twine themselves around the cable, and he pulled them away, holding his body straight up and down a short distance away from the escape line.

"That's funny," he told himself. "I guess I always twined my legs around a rope when I was going down it, so I want to do the same thing going up."

He looked up again quickly and saw legs kicking above him. That would be the pharmacist pulling away from the buoy. How much farther did he have to go? It was hard to judge the distance. He had reached a count of nine, so he should be halfway if he had been putting his hands a foot apart.

His eyes blinked at a form moving up close to him. He saw a man in trunks floating toward him in the water, waving his arms slowly. No, he wasn't waving—he was swimming! He wore a pair of nose clips but no Momsen Lung. One of the instructors from above, March concluded.

The man motioned his arms upward urgently. Unmistakably March knew that he had been going too slowly, so he increased the tempo of his count slightly. And before he knew it, his eyes blinked in the sunlight and he felt water running down his face. He was up!

"Clips off! Valve off!" an instructor in the water beside him said.

March moved away from the buoy toward the side of the tank, where he saw other men standing on the little platform, and as he did so he removed his nose clips with one hand, shut the oxygen valve. Then he remembered that it had not felt a bit strange to breathe through his mouth instead of through his nose.

"I guess as long as your lungs get the oxygen they need, you don't much care how it gets there."

He felt a hand helping him as he climbed up on the little platform at the top of the tower. Standing there, he removed the mouthpiece and then took off the lung itself. As he dried himself and slipped into his robe, the man behind him broke the surface and started toward the edge.

Suddenly March felt a little dizzy. He had looked out the window and had seen how high he was from the ground. And then he smiled.

"What would Scoot think of me?" he thought, "getting dizzy even for a second only a hundred feet off the ground?"

Down below was the river, and March saw a sub making its way down toward Long Island Sound. It looked very tiny and slim.

"How did it go, sir?" asked a voice behind him. He turned and saw the pharmacist.

"All right, I guess," March replied. "Didn't mind it, anyway. I guess I was a little slow. They had to send a man down to hurry me up."

"They sent one down to slow me down," the pharmacist said, "but I came out just about right. They told me it was a better sign if you went too slow than too fast."

"I suppose it indicates you're not overanxious about being under water," March said.

A familiar head broke the water of the tank and March saw Stan Bigelow moving over toward the platform. When he had got out and removed his Lung, he smiled at March.

"Nothing to it, was there?" he called. "I'd like to try the fifty-foot level right away."

"Same here," March said, "but I guess we wait a day or two."

Later, when they *did* make the fifty-foot escape, they found that it went just the same as the eighteen-footer. Sure, it took fifty seconds, but the sensations were about the same. There was more pressure on the ears, but not enough to bother anyone. March was very surprised to hear that one of the enlisted men, near the end of the group, had suddenly gone panicky just before it was his turn to go.

"Had he gone through the eighteen-foot test all right?" March asked the Chief Petty Officer in charge.

"Yes—just too fast," the man replied. "But lots of them do that at first. He must have been holding himself under control for that one, though, and the thought of the fifty was too much for him."

"Too bad," March said. "Will they transfer him back to his old branch of the service?"

"No—they've decided to give him another chance," the Chief said. "The Doc—the psychological one—thinks it's just a fear the guy never even knew he had. He's goin' to talk to him a bit to see if he can find out what caused it. Then maybe he can get rid of it. He won't be able to go down in a pigboat until he handles the fifty-foot escape okay, but we'll keep him on for a while to give him another crack at it. Good man in every other way, as far as I can see."

March learned later that the man was one of the fire controlmen who had ridden out on the bus with him.

"Gee, I hope he makes it," Scott, the radioman, said to March when they talked it over. "He's a swell guy. Cobden's his name, Marty Cobden. And he's got his heart set on bein' a submariner, dreams about it at night even. Never had the faintest notion he was scared of anything, least of all just fifty feet of water."

"Did he go swimming much?" March asked.

"I asked him that, too," Scott replied. "He says he liked to swim but he didn't like to dive. But he wasn't *scared* of it!"

Scott had got over his cold and had caught up with the rest of them, making the eighteen-foot and fifty-foot escapes without difficulty.

"Well, we're qualified now to go to school here," March said. "And we can even go down in a sub. But when do we take the hundred-foot escape?"

"Don't have to," Scott said. "But most of 'em try it, sir—some time later. They all want to see Minnie and Winnie."

"Minnie and Winnie?" March asked. "Who are they and *where* are they?"

"They're mermaids," Scott said without a smile. "Beautiful mermaids. And they're painted on the walls of the tank down at the hundred-foot level. Only one way to see 'em—and that's to make the escape. An' you get a diploma when you've done it."

"I'll see you there, Scott," March said. "We'll both have a look at Winnie and Minnie one of these days."

CHAPTER FIVE

FIRST DIVE

The next day classes started for March and Stan and the other new officers going through the school. Expecting the most difficult and intensive of studies, March was a little disappointed in the first day's work.

"Just ground work, I suppose," he said to Stan at mess that evening. "They couldn't start throwing the whole book at us on the first day."

"I think they did pretty well," Stan said. "I got a big dose of the history and development of the submarine and the construction of modern pigboats. Back in college we'd have taken a week to cover what we got in this one day. But, of course, you've read a lot of general stuff about subs. I was so busy studying engineering in college I didn't look at anything else."

"Yes, I *have* read a good deal about the underwater ships," March said. "I always did think those first experimenters had a lot of guts. Imagine that Dutchman, Van Drebel, submerging a boat more than three hundred years ago."

"Sure, and he stayed down two hours," Stan agreed. "Made about two miles—with oars for power!"

"He must have been a clever guy to have those oars sticking out through leather openings sealed so tight that not a drop of water could come in," March said. "But it was the Americans who really made submarines go."

"Yes—isn't there a ship named after Bushnell," Stan asked, "the man who made that submarine during the American Revolution?"

"Sure, a submarine tender, naturally," March replied. "Too bad his idea didn't work better. It was a clever one."

"I had never realized until today," Stan said, "that Robert Fulton had anything to do with submarines. I thought inventing the steamboat was enough for any one man. But now I find out he invented pretty good submarines long before he did the steamboat. But he just couldn't get anybody to listen to him."

"Well, the sub really couldn't develop into a reliable ship," March said, "until electric motors and storage batteries came along. There were some pretty good attempts, of course, and John Holland and Simon Lake, the two Americans who really made subs that worked, turned out some fair ones driven by gasoline engines, steam engines, and compressed air."

"And don't forget the Diesels!" Stan laughed. "My sweethearts, the Diesels! They were the last things needed, after storage batteries and electric motors, to make subs really dependable and good."

"I won't forget your Diesels, Stan," March said. "I'm going to have to learn plenty about them in the next few weeks, and I know almost nothing now. And you've got to learn plenty about other things, too."

"Sure, it'll be tough going," Stan said. "But it's a wonderful idea to have every officer, no matter what his specialty, able to take over almost any department on a sub if he has to."

"Yes, if I get knocked cold just when we're trying to slip away through some coral atolls to miss a depth-charge attack," March asked, "won't you be glad you really learned how to navigate?"

"Why, all Navy men know how to navigate," Stan protested. "I know my navigation pretty well."

"Maybe so," March agreed, "but do you know it well enough to take a ship a few hundred miles under water without ever a chance to look at the horizon or shoot the sun or get a fix on some landmark? I know I couldn't do it, and navigation's been my main job so far."

"Navigating a sub's no bed of roses, of course," Stan said, "but nursing my pretty Diesels is no easy task, either. When you're workin' on those babies, you pay attention and be good to them."

"I'll be good to your Diesels, all right," March laughed. "But what I'm most anxious to learn about are all the new sound-detection devices. Pretty secret stuff, some of it, though we've had some of it on our surface ships."

"I know," Stan said. "You don't feel so blind and lost in a sub any more, I guess. You can tell from the sound devices just how many ships are near by and even from the sound of their engines what kind they are, where they're goin' and how fast. But you know what I'm anxious to do—really get inside a pigboat and look around. Those cross-section charts are fine, but there's nothing like seeing the real thing for yourself."

"I think they'll be taking us down for a dive within a couple of days," March said. "Just for the ride, you know, and to see how we react. And it had better be pretty soon. That Scoot Bailey has probably been up in a plane half a dozen times at least and I haven't seen the inside of a sub!"

The next morning they looked for an announcement that they would go down in one of the subs but there was nothing of the sort. They spent their time in the classrooms, and they began the really intensive work that March had been expecting.

"One day of preliminary stuff was enough, I guess," he said to Stan at lunch. "They really put us to work this morning."

The classrooms and laboratories of the officer-students were in the same building as those of the enlisted men. Officers and men alike had gone through the same preliminary tests, but now their paths separated. March saw the men regularly, of course, in the halls and around the grounds. He stopped and chatted once in a while with Scott, the radioman, who struck him more and more as a pleasant and serious young man ideally suited to submarine work. He saw the pharmacist, Sallini, and also Marty Cobden, the fellow who had gone to pieces at the fifty-foot level in the escape tower. He was going at his studies like a demon, as if to make up in some way for his one failure to date.

March and Stan saw them that very afternoon again, when they reported, according to instructions, to one of the Chief Petty Officers at the sub base below the school buildings.

"Wonder what's up?" Stan said. "Something for officers and men alike, whatever it is."

"There's only one thing left of that sort," exclaimed March happily. "That's our first pigboat ride! Come on, Stan!"

Stan noticed that there were only about a dozen enlisted men gathered together rather than the whole class.

"Why only some of them?" he wondered.

"Sub won't hold many more, in addition to the regular crew," March said. "And now these boys are really beginning to team up. You know how we've had it drilled into us already that teamwork is the most important part of submarining? Well, they've started to put their teams together. This bunch is a diving section—just enough men for one shift on a sub to handle everything that needs to be handled. They'll work together all through the course, get to know each other, to work well together."

"What if one of the men fails the course?" Stan asked. "There's Marty Cobden, for instance. If he doesn't manage to overcome that fear of the escape tower he's through."

"Then they'll have to replace him," March said. "But that will be just one man out of the section—or maybe two at most will not be able to make it. Well, the majority of the team is still intact. The new man can fit into a well-functioning team pretty fast."

"Will they eventually go out on duty together?" Stan asked.

"Probably," March replied. "When a sub gets three diving sections that have trained together, then it's got a real crew. Of course, they usually try to put in just one new section with two old ones, men who've been through the ropes. The new section, already used to teamwork, fits in with the experienced men well, and learns so much from them that they're veterans after one patrol."

"What about us officers, though?" Stan wondered. "Maybe there's a chance we'll go on the same sub."

"Maybe," March agreed. "They may put two new officers on a sub with three or four veterans. Probably no more, though. Look, here comes the Chief!"

In a few minutes they were all walking down toward the docks where the old O-type submarines used as trainers lay bobbing gently in the waters of the Thames River. March saw that some of the crew were busy about the deck of one of the subs, to which a narrow gangplank led from the dock. As they walked, the Chief Petty Officer was talking to the students.

"When it's in the water," he said, "you can't see much of a sub. The flat deck is just a superstructure built up on top of the cigar-shaped hull. You can see part of the hull itself where the superstructure sides slope down into it. But most of it's under water, where it ought to be on a pigboat."

March's eyes were going over the long slim craft swiftly, not missing a detail. He saw the fins on the side at bow and stern, folded back now, but able to be extended so as to make the planes which could guide the ship up or down. He noted the looming conning tower which served as a bridge for the officers when the pigboat traveled on the surface. From there, he knew, a hatch led down into the center section of the ship. He saw, too, that the fore and aft hatches were open, one leading down into the torpedo room and another into the engine room.

"Look at the deck gun," Stan said. "Wicked looking little thing."

They Watched From the Dock

He pointed to the 3-inch gun mounted on the flat deck forward of the conning tower. It was tightly covered with what appeared to be a canvas cover. March knew that the crew could have that cover off and the gun in action in a matter of seconds.

March and Stan walked across the gangplank and looked up at the officer on the bridge of the conning tower. Saluting, they reported, and received a welcoming smile and the words, "Come on up!"

They scrambled up the ladder and found themselves on the crowded bridge with two other men.

"I'm Lieutenant Commander Sutherland," said the man who had greeted them, "Executive Officer." He turned to the other officer on the deck. "Captain Binkey—Lieutenant Anson and Ensign Bigelow reporting."

The Captain smiled as he returned their salute and then lapsed into his customary informal role.

"Glad to have you aboard," he said. "First ride, eh?"

"Yes, sir," March and Stan replied, feeling at ease at once in the old veteran's presence.

"Sutherland will show you around after we get started," the Skipper said. "I imagine you'll want to stay up here till we're under way."

Sutherland turned to them. "You probably know from your studies what most of this is about," he said. "Just a matter of seeing and feeling it to be at home. I know I don't have to tell you every little detail the way the Chief down there is pointing out every steel plate to those ratings."

March and Stan glanced down to see that the Chief had led his enlisted men on to the deck of the submarine, where they were mingling with the regular crew who were preparing to cast off when the Captain ordered.

"Whenever you want to know anything," Sutherland went on, "just ask me and I'll try to give you the answer. I imagine we'll be casting off in a minute."

They saw the Chief Petty Officer leading his students down the torpedo-room hatch to the interior of the submarine, and for a moment March wanted to join them.

"That will come later," he said. "It's important to see them cast off."

And that operation came without delay. At a word from the Captain, the executive officer began barking orders to the crew and to the enlisted men who stood at the controls on the bridge. The gangplank was taken away by men on the dock, the electric motors began to turn in the ship far below them, and lines were cast off. Slowly, trembling slightly beneath their feet, the pigboat slid back into the river away from the shore, churning up the water only slightly as it moved.

Then suddenly, with a roar, the Diesels caught hold and white smoke poured from the exhaust vents on the sides of the boat. Stan grinned as he heard them, and March said, "Makes you feel at home to hear them, doesn't it?"

"Oh—is he a Diesel man?" Sutherland asked.

"He dreams about them," March replied. "I think he's going to marry a Diesel some day!"

The pigboat was now in the middle of the river and swinging about to head downstream. On the deck below there remained only a few men of the regular crew needed for duties there. March looked around, feeling the thrill of pleasure that always came when a ship set out. The cool breeze fanned his face, and he looked at the shore slipping by, then the buildings of the city. It seemed only a short while before they were in the choppy open water of the Sound. Here there were almost no other ships, and the waters were deep. Soon they would dive!

Below, he knew, the regular crew were at their stations, with the students looking on—each specialist observing the work he would one day do himself. Engine men were in the crowded engine room, peering eagerly at the huge Diesels which powered the ship on the surface. Scott, the radioman, would be standing beside the regular radioman, and Sallini would be going over supplies and equipment of the regular pharmacist, while keeping his eye out for everything else he could learn, too. Every crew member had his special duties, but every one had to be able to take over the duties of any other in an emergency. That was one of the reasons they all liked submarine work, officers and men alike. They learned so much, in so many different fields, in such a short time!

"Rig ship for diving!" said the Captain quietly, and Sutherland, who served also as diving officer, spoke the order into the interphone on the bridge. Throughout the ship below, March and Stan knew, men had sprung to their stations in every compartment. The cook was "securing" the sink, stove, pots and pans. Men at the huge levers controlling the valves of the ballast tanks tested them. The diving planes were rigged out. Below on the deck, the last of the crew slid down the hatches and made them fast from the inside.

Then the reports began to come back over the phone that all was ready inside the boat. An officer in the control room below heard the different rooms of the submarine check in one by one.

"Torpedo room rigged for diving!"

"Engine room rigged for diving!"

When all rooms had reported, the officer below phoned to the Captain on the bridge that the ship was rigged for diving.

"All right, Mister Anson and Mister Bigelow—down you go!"

March quickly moved to the opening and slid down it, his feet reaching for the steps of the straight steel ladder. He was followed at once by Stan and then by Sutherland. Next came the enlisted man who had stood at the controls on the bridge, and finally the Captain himself. The hatch was made fast behind him and everyone was inside the boat.

March glanced around him quickly. And despite the number of drawings and pictures he had seen of the control room of a submarine, he gasped.

Never had he seen such a myriad of instruments and wheels and levers and dials! Everything in the entire submarine was really controlled from this one central room. Beside him, in the middle of the room, were the two thick steel shafts which he knew were the periscopes. Their lower ends were down in wells in the deck and would not be raised until after they were submerged and the skipper wanted to look around.

Facing the bow of the ship, March saw the forward bulkhead of the control room. Yes, there was the huge steering wheel with the helmsman holding it lightly. It seemed strange for a helmsman to be looking at a wall, or instrument panels on a wall, rather than at the open sea over which he steered. March knew that the controls were electrically operated by the wheel and thus easy to handle. But every man was made to steer it by hand on occasion—and that took real strength!—in order to be ready for that emergency that might come when the electric current failed.

Forward, also, were the wheels controlling the angles of the diving planes. There was the gyro-compass dial, and near by the little table at which the navigation officer sat.

"Some day that's where I'll be," March said to himself.

He didn't have time to look carefully at the many other dials against this wall, but he knew they showed the ship's depth under water, the pressure, and other essential data. Along the sides were still more dials showing the amount of fuel in tanks, the number of revolutions per minute being made by the propellers. He recognized the inclinometer, which showed just exactly the angle of tip assumed by the boat in diving or coming up.

On another side were the long levers and wheels controlling the big Kingston valves which flooded the ballast tanks with sea water when the ship was to dive, the air vents, the pumps, and other equipment used in diving and surfacing. The regular crew stood tensely at their posts without a word, and the students who stood near by were completely silent.

March glanced at the Skipper and saw that he was looking at a huge panel on one wall. Yes, this was the "Christmas Tree!" It was a large electric indicator board covered with red and green lights. It showed the exact condition of every opening—hatches, air induction vents, and all—into the ship. Everything having anything to do with diving had its indicator there on the board. March saw that most of the lights were green, but many were still red. He knew that every light had to be green before the ship could dive.

"Stand by for diving," said the Skipper in a quiet voice.

Sutherland, standing behind him, sang out, "Stand by for diving!" The telephone orderly repeated the order over the interphone to all parts of the ship and March jumped as the klaxon horns blared out their raucous warnings. For a moment their sound reverberated in the small steel room, and then Sutherland barked new orders.

"Open main ballast Kingstons!" March saw the men move the levers as he repeated the order, and a few lights turned to green on the "Christmas Tree."

"Stop main engines!" The order was repeated over the phone to the engine room. March felt the trembling of the ship stop as the Diesels were shut off and the electric motors switched on again, taking their current from the huge banks of storage batteries under the deck of the ship. At the same time other lights turned to green on the board.

"Open main ballast vents!" called Sutherland.

One after another the necessary orders were called by the diving officer, they were carried out with precision and reported back at once. Finally, the last red lights on the board winked out as the main air induction valves were closed. Then Sutherland ordered, as the last test, that air be released from the high-pressure tank into the interior of the ship. March watched him look at the dial indicating air pressure within the ship. The hand moved up a little, then held steady. This showed that there was no leakage of air from the boat.

Sutherland turned to the Skipper. "Pressure in the boat—green light, sir."

"Take her down!" said the Captain with a nod.

When the diving officer repeated the order the klaxons blared again their final warning before the diving officer called out one order after another. March had been able to keep close track of everything up to this point, but suddenly, just at the crucial moment, there was too much going on. He heard an order that sounded like "Down bow planes!" and felt the ship tip forward slightly. But at the same time he heard the roar of water as it rushed into the ballast tanks between the inner and outer steel hulls of the ship, the rush of air forced out of the vents by the inrushing water, and the whine of the electric motors.

Sutherland gave an order about the trim tanks which March did not catch, then heard the Skipper say, "Steady at forty feet."

As the order was repeated, March found the dial which indicated the ship's depth and saw the hand approach the forty mark. There the ship leveled out again. The sound of rushing water and bubbling air had ceased and the only sound was the steady hum of the motors.

"We're down!" Stan muttered, almost to himself. March had almost forgotten his companion's existence, but now he turned to him.

"That's right!" he said. "I was so intent on what was happening I almost forgot about that. There's nothing special about it, is there? I mean—being here in this room where you can't see outside—it doesn't make much difference whether you're on top of the water or underneath it."

"Only when I heard the water rushing into the ballasts," Stan answered. "Then I had a little sensation of going under water. It was fast, wasn't it?"

"So fast I couldn't keep track of everything," March replied. "I wonder how long it took from the time the Captain ordered the dive until we leveled off at forty feet."

Sutherland overheard him. "Just sixty-eight seconds!" he said.

CHAPTER SIX

A REAL SUBMARINER

"Scoot Bailey never will have an experience like this as long as he lives!" March said to himself. He was peering through the periscope of the submerged pigboat, looking over the tossing waters of the sea.

When the Captain had called "Up, periscope," the long shaft had moved up by electric motor until the eyepiece and handles were at convenient height. The Skipper had a look around, and March noticed that he turned the handles to adjust the focus.

"Here, have a look, Mister Anson," he said, standing away.

So March had fitted his eyes against the rubber cup and looked. He saw water, a long stretch of open water with nothing on it. It was not completely sharp so he turned one handle slightly, saw the image fuzz up, turned it the other way until it came sharp. Next he moved the periscope around, stepping with it as he did so, looking over the horizon in a sweeping arc.

Then he saw something! It was the shore of Long Island, almost two miles away. He stepped back and said, "I saw the Long Island shore, I think. How far can one see through the periscope, sir?"

"About two and a half miles," the Skipper replied. "Have a look, Mister Bigelow."

Stan stepped forward eagerly to look through the 'scope. He swung it around in a different direction from which March had moved and suddenly exclaimed, "A ship!"

The Captain took over for a look, then said, "Yes, small freighter. Just think how easily we could sink her!"

March looked at the ship. "Looks as though I could knock her down with a BB gun," he said.

"On later trips we'll simulate attacks on some of the ships in the Sound," the Skipper said. "So you'll get a chance to practice something a little more powerful than a BB gun."

For fifteen minutes the pigboat traveled under the water. Sutherland took Stan and March around the control room, explaining the various instruments and levers, answering their questions.

"What beats me, sir," Stan said, "is the number of different things you have to remember! I just can't conceive of doing all that so fast and not forgetting a thing."

"It seems like that at first," Sutherland said. "But after you do it a few times, you get used to it. Just think—driving a car is pretty complicated if you've never even seen a car before. You've got to see the emergency brakes are on, that transmission's in neutral, then turn on ignition, step on electric starter, perhaps choke it a little to start, then push back choke, step on foot throttle, warm up engine, release emergency brake, push in clutch, move gearshift lever, let in clutch, step on throttle, shove in clutch, take foot from throttle, move gearshift lever in another direction, let in clutch and step on throttle for a time, then shove in clutch, take foot from throttle, move gearshift lever, let in clutch, step on throttle again. And all this time, steer the car where you're going, watch out for pedestrians, for traffic lights, for cars behind, for cars on side streets. Why, there are dozens of things you have to do, but when you've driven a car a little while, most of them are almost automatic."

"I'd never though of it that way," Stan said. "But it must take quite a while of handling a dive to get used to it."

"Not so long as you think," Sutherland said, "if you're any good at all. If not, you wouldn't be here. And don't worry—before you leave this school you'll be able to take her down—in three or four different ways—without worrying about it for a second."

The executive officer then led them through the rest of the boat, giving them a quick once-over of the entire ship during their first trip. Stepping over the high door edges of the bulkhead doors leading from one compartment to another, March realized that a fat man would have difficulty getting around on a submarine. He noted how the doors could be fastened watertight and airtight so that any compartment could be sealed off from all the others.

They saw the engine room, with its two banks of heavy Diesels, now quiet and at rest as the ship traveled under water. Stan would have stayed there for the entire trip, talking to the engineers and looking over the power plants, but they moved on to the motor room where the whine of the two electric motors was loud and high-pitched. March knew that the motors could be switched to act as generators driven by the Diesels when the ship surfaced, charging the batteries.

The battery room did not hold their attention for long, although the two banks of huge cells were impressive, but the torpedo room fascinated them. Here was the real reason for the existence of the entire ship, which was nothing more than a vehicle to get the deadly TNT charges into the side of an enemy ship. It was almost the largest of the rooms they had seen, perhaps seeming so because of the additional clear space in the middle. There had to be plenty of room to swing the big torpedoes into position before their tubes.

First March and Stan saw the two racks of torpedoes along the walls. The long cylinders, twenty-one inches in diameter and about twenty feet from end to end, looked deadly. March noted the chain hoist by which they could be swung from their racks into position for loading into the tubes.

The tubes—there were four of them—stuck back into the room a little way, and March and Stan knew they were about twenty-five feet long altogether, their openings at each side just back of the bow of the boat. The tight-fitting doors closed the tubes, and the sub was ready to fire its charges at any moment.

"It must take a terrific blast of air to start these babies on their way," Stan said, running his hand along one of the big torpedoes.

"Yes, it does," Sutherland replied. "But the air doesn't have to move it far. It just expels it from the tube, where there are trigger catches which trip switches here on the torpedo to set its own machinery going."

"Wonderful piece of mechanism, aren't they?" March mused.

"Yes, they're really little submarines with an explosive charge instead of a crew," the executive officer agreed. "And the TNT takes up only a small space, really. Half the length is compressed air to drive the torp. It's got to move pretty fast, you know, to get to the target accurately. There's about four hundred horsepower packed into that little fellow there—from compressed air, heated by an alcohol flame, blowing like fury against two trim little turbines turning the propellers."

"The aiming devices must be very accurate," Stan said.

"Wonderful!" Sutherland exclaimed. "You probably know there's a little whirling gyroscope that keeps the torp on the course which can be set by the operator in advance of firing. Then there's the compensating chamber and pendulum to keep it at its proper depth. It can't very well get off course."

"But don't you have to aim chiefly with the sub itself, sir?" March asked. "I mean—doesn't the sub have to be aimed right at the target for the torpedo to get there?"

"Not at all," Sutherland replied. "The sub doesn't have to be any closer than sixty degrees in facing its target. You set the proper course on the torpedo itself and the automatic devices put it on that course right away— and keep it there!"

"Then the important thing," Stan said, "is for the skipper to get the course right, not necessarily to line up the sub with his target."

"That's right," the older officer agreed. "The skipper must determine the course to his target and call it out. If he's good, he gets his ship."

With a last look around the torpedo room they turned to go back to the control room.

"Later," Sutherland said to them as they stepped through the bulkhead door, "you'll have target practice with special torpedoes that don't blow up what you're aiming at. As a matter of fact, there won't be anything you can't do by the time we get through with you."

They Inspected the Torpedo Room

In the course of the next few weeks, March remembered that statement often. He went on countless trips in the training subs, until he felt as much at home in them as he did in his own quarters. For the first few times he observed. Then he took over one position after another and executed its duties.

Stan was with him on all these trips, but often they were at different ends of the boats during their short journeys. One day, March would take his position at the steering wheel. The next he would handle the big levers controlling the Kingston valves on the main ballast tanks. Then he would work with the men in the engine room, after having studied Diesels in some of his classes. He did a stretch in the torpedo room several times when they shot the practice torps at special targets towed by a surface boat. He worked the interphone system as orderly, took over the little radio shack, spent several hours in the battery room, working the diving planes.

"I've done everything so far but cook lunch and cut the crew's hair," he said to Stan one day, as they relaxed wearily for fifteen minutes after dinner before going to their studies.

"Same here," Stan said. "But I haven't been assistant pharmacist yet."

"Oh, that's right," March recalled. "I haven't passed out any pills yet. And I don't think I'll have to."

"Do you feel that you know the crew's jobs pretty well now, March?" Stan asked.

"Most of them," March replied. "I know I could take over most of them without any trouble. But I'd like another trip or two in the torpedo room, and I want to be at the diving controls for a crash dive before I'll feel sure of myself."

"I agree with you on the diving controls," Stan said, "but I feel okay on the torps now. What I want is a little time on the sound-detector devices."

"You can never have too much time on those," March said. "Every additional hour of experience with them makes you all the better, I think. But it's wonderful that they teach every officer to do every job on the boat—not just the work of the other officers but of every enlisted man on board."

Not only did they handle every job of the crew on the sub, but they spent hours every day in classroom and laboratory. They studied engines and motors and navigation and torpedoes, and—above all, lately—theories of approach and attack. In addition to their work on the training subs themselves, they carried out attack problems in the wonderful "mock-up" control room in one of the buildings. Here was a real control room, with controls and periscopes complete. Standing in position at the 'scope, as if he were the Skipper of the ship, March sighted about on the artificial horizon which looked quite real to him. Suddenly he saw what seemed to be two ships appear on the horizon. First he had to identify them. Then he had to judge their speed and course accurately while they still looked like only tiny spots in his periscopes.

Calling out orders, he directed the course of the "submarine" he was commanding so that he would be in position to fire torpedoes. Then the 'scope went down, as would happen in actual combat. His "sub" was traveling under water, without even the revealing 'scope-ripples to show the enemy where he was. Then he surfaced again, looked through the 'scope to see if he and the "enemy" ships were where they ought to be in relation to each other.

If he was right, he ordered the setting of the torpedo courses and then called "Fire one! Fire two!"

Then he would go over his record with the instructors. He would find out just how well he had done in handling the complete tactical problem that had been presented to him. Had he identified the ships correctly as to nationality, type, size? Had he judged their speed and course correctly? And finally—had his torpedoes hit home? If he had handled the problem correctly, he felt almost the thrill that might have come with sinking an actual enemy ship.

Several afternoons a week, March went out on the training subs. He asked for more time at the diving controls and got it. He asked for two torpedo-room watches and his request was fulfilled. Then he began to take over the duties of the various officers. He served as communications officer, engineering officer, electrical officer, navigation officer—and finally as diving officer. The first time he gave the orders to take the ship down, his heart was in his throat, even though Sutherland was standing by his side to take over at the slightest mistake. He didn't believe that he could possibly remember all the things he had to, but he found, as the orders started coming from his mouth, that his mind ordered them out without his thinking about them. He knew so well, by this time, the logical order of events, that his mind went straight along that path without a hitch.

What pleased March most of all after this experience—even more than the pleasant commendation of the executive officer—was the word spoken to him by Scott, the radioman. Scott had been on the training subs during most of March's trips, too, and they had spoken to each other frequently. But on the dock after March's turn as diving officer, Scott saluted and nodded with a smile.

"If you'll pardon me, sir," he said, "I'd like to mention that you handled that diving like a veteran."

"Thanks, Scott—it's swell of you to say that," March mumbled.

"You know—a bunch of students is likely to get a little funny feeling when we know a new officer's goin' to take us down," Scott said. "But we couldn't have been safer with the Skipper himself than we were with you."

March wrote about that in the letter he wrote to Scoot Bailey that evening. He had been so busy, working hard sixteen hours a day, that Scoot seemed miles and years away.

"I'm beginning to feel like a real submariner at last, Scoot," he wrote. "For a while I thought there was so much to learn that I'd never get there. But I'm at home now, and I think I can make it all right. I suppose you've been feeling much the same way—despite the fact that flying is so much simpler than pigboating—and that you're getting the feeling of being a pilot, without having an instructor in your lap every minute."

CHAPTER SEVEN

ORDERS TO REPORT

Scoot Bailey read March's letter and grinned.

"So flying's easy, he says?" he muttered to himself. "He should have been here going through what I've been through! Aerodynamics, engines, controls, meteorology, gunnery, navigation, bombing, figure-eights, barrel-rolls, spot landings!"

He shook his head and looked at the row of textbooks on the desk before him.

"He's right, though," he said. "I do begin to feel like a flier. At first, before I'd ever been up in a plane, I thought I was one—one of those so-called natural fliers, only there isn't any such thing. Then when I first flew I realized I didn't know much of anything. Next, when I got so I could handle the trainer pretty well, with the instructor right there, I decided flying was pretty simple after all."

He sat back and recalled the day that had changed his mind about that.

"But when he finally told me to take it up alone—boy, oh boy! There I sat in that flying machine with no teacher there to hold my hand. That's when I thought I didn't even know what direction the stick moved, I didn't know which way to push the throttle. What ever gave me the nerve to give her the gun and take off I can never figure out. But when that was over and I was still alive and in one piece, I'd got over the worst of it."

He realized that a submariner had no equivalent of soloing in a plane to go through. He'd have to remember to write that to March.

"After that I straightened myself out," Scoot's thoughts went on. "I wasn't too cocky and I wasn't too scared. I just knew that I had learned to fly a little bit, that there was still a tremendous amount to learn, and that if I worked hard enough I could learn it and turn out to be a pretty good pilot."

Scoot was on the advanced Navy trainer now, a fast ship that came closer in speed and maneuverability to the fighters he would eventually fly.

"In another week I'll be heading for the training carrier," he said with a glow of satisfaction. "I'll get my wings and I'll be a real Navy pilot, but I've still got a lot to learn. Taking off from those heaving decks—and landing on 'em again—is going to be quite different from the same moves on these nice flat Texas plains."

As Scoot thought about it, about the work March had been doing, he realized that there was a great deal in common in their fields. Flying a plane wasn't much like handling a submarine, but both of them got away from the normal positions of most people. The flier got away from the earth's surface in one direction. The submariner got away from it by going under. They both handled craft that could travel in a three-dimensional sphere, not just over the surface like a tank or a battleship.

"March practices coming up with a Momsen Lung," Scoot told himself, "while I practice coming down with a parachute. That Lung's just a sort of underwater parachute."

A plane was just a vehicle to get explosives into position for firing at the enemy and so was a submarine, Scoot concluded. And sometimes they even handled the same explosives—torpedoes!

"Now if someone would just invent a flying submarine," Scoot thought, "March and I could get together again. But I guess that's not very likely outside the comic strips. When you think of the terrific water pressure a sub has to stand, you can't very well imagine hooking wings on to something that heavily plated with steel. And think of the batteries! No—I'm afraid March and I will be separated for some time. It seems a shame, though, sub and plane ought to make a mighty fine team."

The next week, as Scoot started off from Corpus Christi for the training carrier off the shores of Florida, March was setting off on one of the most important underwater trips of his training. It was a trip of two days on which March was to act throughout as navigation officer, still his specialty despite his training in every other job on the ship. March knew his navigation thoroughly while he was still on surface ships, but with the intensive extra study he had gone through at New London, especially on dead reckoning and "blind" navigation for underwater travel, he was a master.

During the trip, on which Stan Bigelow also acted as engineering officer in charge of the Diesels and motors, they got the real feeling of being on patrol. They simulated traveling through enemy waters and so ran submerged most of the daylight hours, the Skipper taking a look around occasionally with the periscope.

Numerous drills were also rehearsed during the voyage—fire drills, man-overboard drills, crash dives. They simulated a chlorine gas danger, acting as if the sea water had got into the batteries to give off the deadly fumes. Gas masks were out in a hurry and the battery room was sealed off with only two "casualties."

"The only thing we haven't tried on this trip," March said at mess the first evening, "is some of the first aid we've learned."

"Well, if someone will volunteer to simulate appendicitis," the Skipper laughed, "I'm sure Pills will try an operation. But you forgot something else we haven't tried—a depth-charge attack."

"I'd just as soon skip that, sir," Stan said, "at least until the real thing hits me."

"No way of simulating it, anyway," the Captain commented. "But it's about the only thing we leave out in this training."

"There's one big difference," March said. "In training, if you make a mistake, why you just get a bad mark from the teacher. In real submarining in war time, you're likely to get—dead. And carry a lot of others along with you."

"What do you mean?" the Skipper asked. "That's true at the beginning, of course, but not now. You're really navigating this boat, Mr. Anson. Nobody else is doing it, and nobody's checking up on you. If you do it wrong, we'll pile up on Montauk Point!"

March gulped. And Stan looked a little worried.

"What's the matter, Stan?" March asked. "Are you scared? Think I'm not a good enough navigator?"

"No, I was just wondering," Stan said, "if the same thing applied to me— if I'm really totally responsible for all these engines on this trip."

"Of course you are, Mr. Bigelow," the Skipper smiled. "And I'm sure you'll handle them very nicely, just as I'm confident Mr. Anson will take us just where we're supposed to go. You are not allowed to take over these duties until you have proved conclusively, in your previous work, that you could do so."

As darkness descended over the waters of Long Island Sound, the training sub surfaced and found herself just where she was supposed to be at that time, much to March's relief. Hiding behind a point of land near the end of Long Island, they charged their batteries, while a skeleton crew stayed on watch. Most of the others went to bed for a few hours' sleep in the bunks which lined the walls of most of the rooms. March and Stan shared a tiny cabin, but were not in it at the same time, as their watches followed one another.

Before dawn the next morning the sub set off from its cove, submerged, and followed the next course under water. Sending up the periscope at about ten o'clock, the Skipper saw the target boats at the designated spot and the sub went through a series of simulated attacks on enemy shipping, crash diving to get away from "destroyers" attacking them, lying on the bottom with all motors shut off for a spell, then sneaking away at a depth of two hundred feet in a circuitous course to outwit the enemy waiting for them.

During all the trip the Skipper and Lieutenant Commander Sutherland were closely observing, without seeming to do so, the actions of March and Stan, and of the student diving section which had shipped with them for this special trip. They were interested in seeing not just whether the men could handle their jobs, but *how* they did it—if calmly or with too much tension. On occasion one or the other of the two senior officers would give a conflicting order or misunderstand something reported by Stan or March, just to see what happened. Not once did Stan or March become upset, and the two older men smiled at each other meaningly.

The Sub Set Off and Submerged

"Two good officers," the Skipper said. "I wish I could get out on patrol again and take along a couple of new young men like that."

"I'd go anywhere with them myself," said Sutherland. "Why do we have to be so old, Skipper?"

"Didn't you have enough action in the last war?" the Captain asked.

"No, sir, and neither did you!"

"Well, men like Anson and Bigelow will have to do it for us this time, I guess," the Captain said. "And I suppose we're doing an important job if we help at all to make them such good pigboat officers."

"They're ready to be assigned now, don't you think?" Sutherland asked.

"Yes, without a doubt. They can't learn any more except through actual experience. They might as well start getting it right away."

March and Stan felt sure that their training was coming to an end. So far as classes were concerned, they knew that they had covered just about all the work that the school had to give them. They had studied so hard that they felt mentally exhausted.

"I don't think I could cram one more fact into my head," Stan said. "It's going to take some time for the facts I've been putting in there to assemble themselves and settle down in some orderly fashion."

"We'll be leaving before long," March said. "But there's one thing I want to do before I leave. I want to see Winnie and Minnie."

"Oh—in the escape tower?" Stan exclaimed. "Of course—we've never made the hundred-foot escape."

"We don't have to, but just about everybody does," March said. "Want to do it with me tomorrow?"

"Sure, if there's a group going through," Stan agreed. "By the way, what happened to that fellow Cobden who flubbed the fifty-foot escape?"

"He made it," March said. "And he's already done the hundred-footer, too. The psychiatrist found out what was bothering him. When he was just a kid he was swimming with a gang and one of 'em ducked him and held his head under water a bit too long. He got some water in his lungs, passed out, but they revived him. He'd forgotten all about it, really—except underneath, of course. He said that later when he made up his mind to learn how to swim well, it took a lot of grit to make himself do it. He didn't know why it bothered him, but he had the guts to fight it out and really learn how to swim. Never did any diving, though—didn't like being completely under water."

"And after all these years that old experience pops up!" Stan exclaimed.

"It just goes to prove that all these tests are so sensible!" March said. "What if he hadn't found that out until he got in a sub on duty somewhere? His going to pieces then might have wrecked it, or caused plenty of trouble."

"He's all over it now?" Stan asked.

"Sure," March said. "As soon as the doc got the story out of him and explained it, Cobden just laughed and said he felt foolish. Went right over to the fifty-foot level and did the escape. He even joked with the Chief and said that he shouldn't hold his head under water—it might make a neurotic out of him."

"That's swell!" Stan commented.

"Yes, and he insisted on taking the hundred-foot escape right away, too," March went on. "But they were smart. They wouldn't let him. They thought he might be acting under a temporary fit of courage and bravado and the old fear might come back on him later. So they made him wait a couple of weeks. It went fine, though."

Before going to the escape tower the next day, March looked up Scott, the radioman, and reminded him of their date to look at Winnie and Minnie together. So Scott and March and Stan went to the hundred-foot tower together that afternoon, donned their swimming trunks, their Momsen Lungs, and stepped under the metal skirt in the water at the bottom. As March started up the long cable leading to the surface, he realized that the hatch and platform there were made exactly like the top of a real sub. And there on the walls were the two beautiful mermaids, Winnie and Minnie, smiling at him. He could not smile back, because of the Momsen Lung mouthpiece, but he waved at the girls and went slowly up past them.

At the fifty-foot platform an instructor swam out and around him, waving his arms to indicate that March was moving up at the correct speed. As he broke the surface he felt fine, as if one of the last acts at New London had been accomplished. Stan and Scott followed him quickly, and then the three of them were presented with the special diplomas, decorated with pictures of Winnie and Minnie, stating that they had made the hundred-foot escape.

As March and Stan walked back to their quarters, March said, "Now I feel ready for anything!"

And waiting for him were his orders—to report in two weeks to Baltimore, Maryland, for duty aboard the new submarine, *Kamongo*.

CHAPTER EIGHT

KAMONGO

"*Kamongo?*" Stan exclaimed, holding in his hands the orders which directed him to the same ship. "What kind of fish is that?"

"Never heard of it," March said. "They're building so many subs these days that they're running out of fish to name them after. Let's ask the Exec tonight at mess."

Captain Sampson knew about the Kamongo.

"A very important creature," he said. "If there hadn't been a Kamongo, we probably wouldn't be here today."

"What do you mean, sir?" Stan asked, wondering at the officer's smile and twinkling eyes.

"Well, the story has to go very far back in history," the Captain said, "back when the earth was mostly covered with water and the only living creatures were *in* the water. There had to be something that crawled out of the water and learned how to live on land. That was Kamongo."

"How did he do it?" March asked. "Did he have lungs?"

"Maybe a Momsen Lung," Stan suggested with a laugh.

"Not quite." Captain Sampson smiled. "We don't know that it was Kamongo itself that did the crawling out, but it must have been something like him. You see, another name for Kamongo is Lungfish. He's a kind of fish—more fish than anything else in many ways—but he's also got lungs of a sort. He can live under water or above it. And so can a submarine. I think it's a fine name for a sub. I'd like to be boarding her with you."

"*Kamongo,*" muttered Stan, almost to himself. "*Kamongo.*"

"Yes, I've been thinking the same thing," March said. "Getting used to our ship's name. It's like suddenly finding out you've got a wife and somebody tells you her name—and you've never heard it before."

"If you say it over more and more," Stan said, "you get to like it. It's got a good sound."

"Yes, I think so," March agreed. "It's got strength. And for some reason it sounds sleek and trim. And being able to live above or below the water— that's our ship, all right!"

"Two weeks," Stan mused. "You're going home, I suppose?"

"Yes, I'm going home," March replied. "It may be the last time for quite a spell."

"I'm going, too," Stan said. "Good old Utica, New York. I'm glad it isn't far."

So Stan and March said goodbye the next day, as they said goodbye to all the others they had come to know so well at New London. But to each other they were able to say, "See you in a couple of weeks—aboard *Kamongo!*"

Then March went home, and saw his mother and Scoot's family and many of his old friends. But Hampton did not seem right without Scoot himself. It had been a wrench when he went off to New London without him, but there he had been so busy, so absorbed, that he had hardly had time to miss his friend of so many years. Now, back in the town they had grown up in together, the town wasn't all there without Scoot.

March had written Scoot a note before leaving New London, telling him that he was going home on leave before reporting for duty. And Scoot had gnashed his teeth on getting the letter, realizing that March had finished his training first. Scoot felt that he was finished, too, for he had done everything but fly down the funnel of the training carrier—backwards.

"What's left for me to learn?" he asked. "Unless they set up some real Jap Zeros here for me to shoot at I don't see what else I can do."

Then, just four days before March had to leave Hampton, Scoot got his own orders—to report in three weeks' time to the new aircraft carrier *Bunker Hill* at San Francisco!

He raced home from Florida as fast as he could go, and he and March had two days together before March left. They talked submarines and airplanes all day and all night, and Scoot's family had to wait until March left before they had a really good chance to visit with him.

But March felt better when he got on the train for Baltimore. It was good to have seen Scoot for even that short time. There were a million other things they could have talked about, but they had got close to one another again in that time and they had gained greater spirit from their companionship.

He tried not to think that he might not see Scoot again—ever. But he couldn't help facing it.

"After all," he told himself, "submarine duty is no bed of roses. People do get killed in it. And flying a Navy fighter against the Japs is not the safest occupation in the world. There are lots of young fellows going out on such jobs who won't be coming back from them. How do I know but what Scoot and I—or one of us, anyway—are among them?"

But such thoughts did not stay with him long. No matter what the facts of the matter or the statistics of casualties in wartime, March felt very confident of returning home safe and sound and going on to live to be at least ninety-five. As the train rolled along ever nearer to Baltimore, he thought more and more of *Kamongo*, his new home, his new ship on which he was to be the navigation officer.

"She's probably about 1500 tons," he said, "like most of them they're building now. Trim and neat, about three hundred and some odd feet long. She'll have one three-inch deck gun and a couple of antiaircraft machine guns. Eight or ten torpedo tubes—fore and aft."

He tried to picture *Kamongo* in his mind, so much more modern and powerful than the old O-boats on which he had been training.

"Air-conditioned," he mused. "All the new ones are. I'm lucky to get on a brand-new ship! Freshwater showers. Plenty of refrigeration for carrying good food. Why, we'll probably come up with turkey on Christmas Day!"

He pictured his life in the submarine, his meals, his quarters.

"I may have a little cabin of my own—not much more than a telephone booth, but all mine. Maybe not, of course, but these new ones really make you comfortable. Probably five officers aboard, crew of about fifty-five or sixty."

He wondered where they would go, where they would hunt out the enemy ships.

"Reporting on the Atlantic doesn't mean anything," he said. "That's just where she'll take the water after her trials. We may take her anywhere for action. Now, Scoot knows he'll be serving in the Pacific. He wouldn't be going to San Francisco otherwise. Of course, most subs are in the Pacific now, too, but there are plenty operating in the Atlantic. Can't tell where we'll go. But we'll have a cruising range of about fifteen thousand miles. We can go just about anywhere we want."

And then he thought of Stan. He liked the young Ensign with whom he had gone through school at New London. He didn't, of course, feel as close to him as he did to Scoot. There wasn't the same warmth between them. But the busted-nosed redhead was a real man, intelligent, human, and a good friend.

"I'll be darned glad to get on that boat and find one familiar face," March told himself. "I wonder what the Skipper's like."

He began to think more and more of this after he got off the train and headed for the Navy Yard. If the Skipper happened to be an old-timer contemptuous of youngsters, or a gruff sort without any heart in him—then it might not be so good. As he approached the gate, and prepared to show the sentry his pass, he saw someone ahead of him that looked familiar.

"Stan!" he called, still not sure that it really was Bigelow. And then, as the man turned, he was sure he had been wrong, for the man wore the stripes of a Lieutenant (j.g.) and Bigelow was only an Ensign.

But the man called back "March!" and March knew his first guess had been right. It *was* Stan Bigelow!

"Stan!" he cried, pumping his hand vigorously. "I thought I was wrong. They've finally found out how good you are and made you a Lieutenant!"

"Sure!" Stan cried. "The only thing that bothered me was that I ought to have been made an Admiral. It all happened during my leave. I was sure sick of being an Ensign. Do you remember how the CPO's look down on an Ensign?"

"I surely do!" March said, showing his papers to the sentry. "But they don't think junior Lieutenants are so wonderful, either, as you'll soon find out."

"But I think Chief Petty Officers are wonderful," Stan said. "They know more than half the Rear Admirals in the Navy."

They were walking along the path together, between long low buildings. For a few minutes they said nothing.

"Gee, I'm glad I ran into you," Stan said.

"I was just thinking the same thing," March said with enthusiasm. "I'm excited as the devil about this, but I began to feel the need of a friend close at hand. I wonder what the Skipper will be like."

"Are you reading my thoughts?" Stan exclaimed. "He can make or break us, you know."

"I know it!" March replied. "Why, on this first cruise the commanding officer can get us out of the sub service just by saying he doesn't like the color of our eyes."

"They've Made You a Lieutenant!"

"Well, we're going to find out pretty soon," Stan said. "That looks like a mighty pretty pigboat alongside that dock up ahead. It might be ours."

It *was* theirs. It was *Kamongo*, long and sleek and beautiful in the dark waters that lapped her sides. They showed the necessary papers to the guard at the gangplank and went aboard. It was now almost completely dark.

"Everybody's down below," March said.

"Skipper may not even be there," Stan replied.

The sentry overheard them. "The Skipper's below, sir," he said.

March and Stan walked across the narrow gangplank, climbed the conning tower ladder and then slid down the hatch to the control room below. It was brilliantly lighted, and they looked around, blinking.

First of all March saw the gleaming, shining, newness of everything in the room. It was beautiful! Then his eyes focused on two or three crewmen who looked casually at him, then on a young man, about his age, who looked up with a smile. He saw the Lieutenant's (not j.g.) stripes and saluted.

"Lieutenant Anson, sir, reporting," he said.

"Lieutenant Bigelow," Stan echoed him.

The young man saluted back casually.

"Hello," he said. "Glad to know you. My name's Gray."

March smiled. He liked this young man right away. Maybe another new officer.

"We'd like to report to the Skipper," he said in a friendly tone.

"You've done it, men," the man said lightly. "I'm the Skipper."

March was thunderstruck. This young fellow the Skipper? Why, he didn't look any older than March or Stan, and March knew that *he* wasn't qualified to be the Captain of a submarine. But he quickly abandoned his friendly tone and grew formal.

"Oh—yes, sir," he said. "Lieutenant Anson reporting."

"So you said," the Skipper replied. "Come on into my quarters."

He turned and led the way through the small bulkhead door to a narrow hall from which doors led to very small cabins. In the first of these he turned and sat down behind a small table.

"Officers' mess," he said, motioning them to sit down. "Cramped but beautiful. Make yourselves at home."

Stan and March didn't know what to say. They liked the young man, but their surprise at his youth bothered them. He seemed to sense their thoughts, and smiled.

"Don't be upset," he said. "I'm not quite as young and inexperienced as I look. Graduated from Annapolis six years ago, been in submarines ever since. I was executive officer on the *Shark* in the Pacific since the war began— happened to be at Pearl Harbor when it happened. On my last patrol lost my Skipper—God bless him—when he had a heart attack. Had to take over. Transferred to this new baby when I got back. Now—where do you come from?"

March relaxed and smiled. He liked this man at once. He could see their thoughts, their surprise, and he could put them at their ease at once.

"Served a year aboard the *Plymouth*," he said. "Volunteered for submarine duty, sent to New London, just completed training there."

"My story doesn't sound so good," Stan said. "I was a teacher—and I didn't like it. Diesels, mainly. They finally gave in because I pestered them so much and sent me to New London. I went through the mill there with March—er, Lieutenant Anson."

"We might as well get this name business out of the way," Gray said. "I'm not one for rushing into calling everybody by his first name right off, but on the other hand I don't believe in keeping up the formalities forever—especially on a submarine. My name's Larry. When you feel you know me well enough and it comes easy, call me that. Until then, call me Skipper or Gray."

"My name's March Anson," March said.

"It must have been bad when you were an Ensign," Gray said. "A lot of puns about Ensign Anson, I'll bet."

March grinned. "Plenty," he replied. "That was the reason I liked my promotion so much."

"I don't know why I liked it," Stan said. "But I just got mine and I'm mighty happy about it. Anyway, my name's Stan."

"Now, we're straight on that," Gray said. "Anson, you're the navigation officer, according to my reports, and Bigelow is the engineering officer. There are two others. You'll meet them a little later in the evening. Corvin is my Exec. He was with me on the *Shark*. He's the diving officer, too. McFee was another from the *Shark*—he's communications and handles commissary on the side. Bigelow, you may not know, but you'll take care of the electrical end of things as well as engines."

"Yes, sir," Stan said, hoping inwardly that he would remember all he had learned about the many electrical ends of the submarine. "Electricity's everything on a sub!"

"Well, not quite everything," Gray smiled. "But it's pretty important. We can't get along very well without it, anyway. But if you need any advice or just plain moral support, get next to McFee. He knows electricity backward and forward."

There was a moment's silence. Then Gray showed them to their quarters. Stan and March shared a tiny cabin that looked like a palatial mansion to them at once because they loved it so much. Then the Skipper asked if they had eaten dinner before they came aboard. They had not.

"Good!" Gray said. "I'm just about to eat. We'll have it together."

They went back to the little room that served as officers' mess and the messboy appeared. Within a few moments they were eagerly eating rare roast beef, French fried potatoes, succotash, with biscuits and hot coffee.

"Don't get spoiled by the biscuits," Gray said. "We eat pretty well, but the cook doesn't have time for such frills very often when we're under way."

By the time the meal was over March and Stan felt completely at home, and Gray seemed very much at ease.

"We'll go over the ship tomorrow morning," he said. "She's a beauty. Nothing finer being built today, and I know you'll love *Kamongo*. Know about her name, by the way?"

"Yes, Captain Sampson told us about it when we got our orders in New London," March said. "I like it."

"So do I," Stan said. "I felt proud telling everybody at home about what it meant."

A little later, while they were talking, Corvin and McFee, the two other officers, came in together. Introductions were informal and easy, and March began to feel very happy. These two men were just as young as their Skipper. March felt as if he were really at home with people just like himself. He turned and gave a look at Stan, who was beaming.

"What's that mean?" Gray asked, who seemed to notice everything. "Think you'll like us?"

March didn't know what to say. "It's hardly up to us to decide—" he began.

"Oh, yes, it's very important," Gray said. "If I don't like you—off you'll go. If you don't like me—I'll know it, even if I like you, and off you'll go anyway."

He laughed. "You see, we've got to get along together."

McFee spoke up. "I think we will, Larry."

They talked for two hours more before going to bed. Gray told them that the rest of the crew would report the next morning before eight, and that they'd get under way by noon.

March slept the sleep of the good and the happy, dreaming only of navigating *Kamongo* right into the Japanese emperor's back yard, in which he proceeded to sink the entire Japanese Imperial Navy.

The next morning the officers had breakfast together, except for Corvin, who had stood watch in the early morning hours and so was sleeping. They all went into the control room then, where March was startled to see a familiar face.

"Scott!" he cried.

"Yes, sir!" cried the radioman with a wide smile. "I'm certainly happy to see *you*, sir!" And then he saw Stan behind March. "And you, too, *Lieutenant* Bigelow!"

"You notice things pretty quickly, don't you, Scotty?" Stan laughed.

"You've got to, sir, if you're in submarines!"

"Did you know you'd be assigned here, Scott?" March asked.

"Not when you left, sir," Scott replied. "And then I didn't know where you'd been assigned. We're all here, you know—the whole diving section that worked together at New London—Cobden, and Sallini, and all of us."

"Wonderful!" March cried. "Why, I feel completely at home already!"

"So do I, sir!" Scott said.

Gray, who had listened to the exchange of conversations, spoke up.

"The Navy is wonderful!" he said. "They really do things right. You'd think nobody higher up would have time to think of these things. But here we've got two-thirds of a crew with officers that've been in action. And the other third, just trained, all know each other. Officers and men were trained together. Why, we're really going to get along."

As they went through the ship, March and Stan said hello to the other men of the diving section from New London, and there were mutual congratulations all around. A spirit of happiness and friendship spread through the boat. The older crew members, most of whom had served under Gray before, caught this spirit and felt that all this was a good sign, a good omen for a new ship just starting out on her shakedown cruise. March saw Gray close his eyes for a moment, and smile very slightly. He suddenly realized the Skipper's great responsibilities. He knew that a crew that got along was essential to successful submarine work. And it had happened. This crew was going to click, and Gray knew it. He was duly thankful!

CHAPTER NINE

DESTINATION—

All during the morning supplies were being loaded into *Kamongo*—food and oil and water and torpedoes. Larry Gray spent the time from eleven to eleven forty-five at Navy headquarters, going over final details and receiving his sealed orders. When he returned, his officers reported to him one by one, informing him that their departments were ready.

He looked at his watch. "Fine," he said. "We might as well shove off. Come on, Ray." He stepped from his quarters into the control room with Corvin, his executive officer, behind him. There he saw March at the little navigation desk.

"Want to come up to the bridge with us?" he asked. "We're getting under way."

"Sure thing," March replied. "I might as well wave goodbye to land. We may not see any for some time."

"Oh, I think we'll be seeing land for a while," Gray replied, starting up the ladder to the conning tower.

"Oh—you know where we're going?" March asked.

"No, but I've got my ideas," the Skipper answered.

Ray Corvin grinned at March as he stepped up the ladder. "And his ideas are usually right," he muttered.

On the bridge, March looked over the busy waters of the harbor. A gray mist hung over everything, penetrating sweaters and coats in a chilling wave. March shivered.

"Well, now that winter's coming on," he said, "I hope you're leading us to a warmer climate."

"I think so," said Gray, as his eyes swiftly went over his boat, the dock, and the ships in the harbor. "But you never can tell. It might be Iceland or the run to Murmansk."

"Brrr!" shivered Ray Corvin. "Don't mention it."

"Okay, Ray, let's get going," Gray said, and Corvin began to bark his orders for casting off the lines. March knew that Stan Bigelow was below looking over his shining new Diesels, ready for the moment when they would roar into action. After all the training he had gone through—this at last was the real thing. He had to make those Diesels run and run right at all times.

This was a shakedown cruise, but it was probably combined with the voyage of getting to some battle zone. March and Stan were not full-fledged submarine officers quite yet—not for sure. This first assignment was their last test. If they did a good job and pleased the Skipper they'd be set. If not—they'd be out!

The electric motors whined as the pigboat slid back away from the dock into open water. Then came the roar of the Diesels and the clouds of white smoke from the exhaust vents, and March smiled, knowing Stan's pride in the powerful rumble of those engines. In a few minutes the boat had swung around and headed downstream toward Chesapeake Bay. For some time, they knew, they would be traveling between two long shores. Here they could easily go on the surface, but once out in the open sea they would have to travel submerged during daylight hours.

It had surprised March when he first learned that our own subs traveled submerged in our own waters. But when he came to think of it, it made sense. There were German subs traveling in our waters, too, and there was a constant naval and aerial patrol looking for them. From the air, the markings on a pigboat did not stand out very well, particularly if a rolling sea were breaking over it. And the anti-sub patrol had orders to shoot first and ask questions later. A German sub could crash-dive very quickly when sighted and the minute or two taken to look more closely or to ask questions might result in its escape.

After half an hour Larry Gray went below, leaving March and Ray Corvin on the bridge with two enlisted men, one serving as lookout and the other handling the controls. March had little to do until they were in the open sea, for navigating down the Bay was no job at all. After they were out a few hours the Skipper would open his sealed orders and then March would have a job to do, charting the sub's course to their destination.

He and Corvin talked with each other, leaning on the rail and watching the choppy waters slide past the sleek sides of *Kamongo*. Ray spoke of Larry Gray with such warmth of feeling, such admiration, that March felt sure of his own first impression of the Skipper. Here was a man he would like, and would grow to like more and more as time went on.

"It's cold," Corvin said. "Why don't you go below and have a cup of coffee? Nothing going on here."

"Guess I will," March said. "See you later."

March slid down the ladder to the control room and started over to the officers' wardroom. Then he saw Scotty at the little radio shack and stopped to speak with him.

"How do you feel, Scotty?" he asked. "It's good to get going, isn't it?"

"I should say so, sir," Scott replied. "Know where we're going?"

"Not yet," March replied. "Skipper opens orders ten hours out."

"Well, wherever we're going," Scott said, "I'm sure glad we're goin' with you, sir. And the whole gang feels the same way. You see, we sort of liked the way you handled the pigboats back there in New London."

"Thanks, Scotty," March said. "And you don't know how good it made me feel to find you boys here. Bigelow and I felt right at home from then on."

March turned and found the Skipper at the door, smiling.

"Come on in for a cup of coffee," Gray said.

"Thanks," March replied, sliding down behind the little table in the wardroom with Gray.

"Jimmy just brought the pot of coffee," Gray said, filling March's cup. "It's hot. Jimmy's the messboy, by the way—nice kid."

March smiled to himself. Jimmy the messboy was only about one year younger than Gray.

"Those men you knew in New London," Gray said, "seem to like you."

"We got to know each other pretty well," March said. "We went through the whole business together. There are some swell men among them."

"What about Sallini, the pharmacist?" Larry asked.

"Fine—one of the best," March said. "He's quiet and reserved, serious-minded, but with a nice sense of humor you don't always suspect is there."

"I like that kind," Gray said. "I was a little hesitant about having a new pharmacist on board. It can be a mighty important job if there's serious sickness or trouble. Think he can stand the gaff?"

"I think he'd get better the more difficult the situation," March said. "One of the prizes of the bunch is that Cobden. He really has guts."

March told the Skipper about Cobden's experience with the escape tower and his overcoming of his emotional fears.

The Skipper Was at the Door

"That's swell," Gray commented. "Nothing much can lick anybody after that. With our Chief in the torpedo room, Kalinsky, the man ought to turn into a real submariner. Pete Kalinsky is one of the best men in the whole Navy. Men under him love him, and they learn plenty, too."

March looked up as the red head and bulldog face of Stan Bigelow appeared. He sat down and joined them in a cup of coffee. The engineering officer was smiling broadly.

"Did you ever hear anything prettier than those engines?" he demanded.

"Well—the Philharmonic is pretty good," March laughed, "and I think I prefer Bing Crosby."

"Not me!" Stan exclaimed. "That purr is the sweetest sound there is. And are those beauties! The very latest thing, you know, the very latest!"

"I personally ordered them that way," Gray smiled. "And I'm glad you're satisfied. I never liked an engineer that didn't have a deep and abiding affection for his engines."

After talking a while, March went to the chartroom and went through the detailed maps idly, picking out one here and there that looked interesting to him.

"Celebes—Pago-Pago—Ceylon—and look at this, Wake Island! Some of those names sound wonderful. Wonder if we'll hit any of them."

Later he went up to the bridge again and found that Larry Gray had relieved Corvin.

"I feel sort of useless," he said. "Nothing to do yet."

"Nothing much for any of us to do right now," Gray said. "Plain sailing like this isn't very hard. Most of the crew are lying down, reading, playing checkers or just shooting the breeze. Why don't you have a little rest?"

"Not I," March said. "Not on my first day out. I don't want to miss anything. Anyway, in another hour we ought to be getting away from land a bit, and a couple of hours after that you'll be opening your orders. I want to know where we're going just as soon as I can."

As the time approached for opening the orders, there was an air of tenseness throughout the boat. The crew members who had been lying down weren't sleepy or tired any more. They were up, walking back and forth in the narrow passageways, climbing up the forward hatch for a breath of fresh air, climbing down again to get another cup of coffee. Everyone but Larry Gray seemed a little nervous. He still stood calmly on the bridge, looking out over the long rollers in which *Kamongo* now sailed. The last line of land had finally disappeared behind them.

He glanced at his watch, and then slid down the conning tower hatch without a word. McFee and Corvin and March Anson, who were all on the bridge with him, looked at each other.

"This is really my watch," McFee said. "Go on down, you two, but for gosh sakes let me know as soon as you find out."

So March and Ray Corvin went below and sat down in the wardroom. They knew the Skipper was in his quarters next door.

"He'll be calling for the chart in a minute," Corvin said. "The chart of where we're going. Then we'll know."

But Gray did not call for a chart. Instead, he sauntered into the wardroom sat down and smiled.

"Sorry to disappoint you," he said. "I feel a little let down myself, though it's a perfectly natural destination."

"Not Iceland!" Corvin cried. "Don't tell me that!"

Gray laughed. "No, our present destination is just a way-station."

"Well, if it's so all-fired disappointing," Corvin exploded, "why are you trying to build it up into something dramatic by holding out on us? I think it's just a gag. It's probably that we're going to blast Kiel harbor from inside or find some way of traveling up the sewers to Paris."

"Ray, you've been going to too many movies," Larry said. "You know that life on a submarine is very prosaic, except for just once in a while. Gentlemen, we are going to San Francisco, California!"

CHAPTER TEN

THROUGH THE CANAL

It had been a bad anticlimax! Everybody in the crew felt badly let down. Corvin and March forgot all about telling McFee, up on the bridge, who was mentally trying to decide between the Marshall Islands and the Black Sea as probable destinations. Finally he phoned down and angrily asked why someone didn't let the bridge know where they were supposed to be going.

"How do you expect anybody to steer the ship in this big ocean," he demanded, "if he doesn't know where he's going?"

When he heard the words "San Francisco," he groaned.

"What's the matter with San Francisco?" Stan asked. "I've always wanted to see it."

"Oh—San Francisco's wonderful," Ray Corvin said "As a matter of fact I live not far from there, and maybe I'll get a chance to see my family for a day or two, so I'm very happy in some ways. It's just that we got so keyed up expecting to head right into a pitched battle."

"I'm not too surprised," Gray said. "I felt sure we were going to the Pacific and I thought we might go direct to our base there. But if we hit Frisco on the way—that's only natural. Of course, we'll get more orders there and then we'll surely head for some action."

March felt just as well about the news. He would have a chance to learn everything about the submarine from one end to the other. He would actually navigate the ship a few thousand miles, but without having to worry too much about enemy ships or mines or planes while doing it. By the time they left San Francisco he'd feel like a veteran submariner. He would be able to handle his regular tasks without thinking about them, and he'd be able to take actual fighting with vigor and enthusiasm.

During the daytime they ran submerged a good deal of the time, taking a look through the periscope occasionally. Once the Skipper saw a U.S. Navy blimp right above them and they headed for two hundred feet depth in a hurry. But nothing happened.

At night they ran on the surface, and they were lucky enough to have good weather most of the time, with plenty of stars for March to shoot on the sextant so that he could check his course. He was pleased to see that his instrument navigation, carried out when they were submerged, was checked by his celestial observations.

There came a day that was cloudy and overcast, so the Skipper decided to travel on the surface.

"There won't be any planes out today," he said. "And we can make much better time on top. But keep a sharp lookout for other surface craft. Can't see very far in this fog."

March took over his regular watch that afternoon on the bridge. He had on a heavy sweater and waterproof hood and jacket, for the moisture in the air, even if it were not rain, soaked everything inside of fifteen minutes. Two crew members were on lookout, in addition to the man at the controls. March listened to their regular calls of "All clear" and stared ahead into the blanket of fog.

Then, suddenly, he saw it—just as the lookout shouted.

"Freighter on port bow!"

March shouted the alarming news into the interphone, ordered the man at the controls to reverse engines full-speed and put her over hard starboard. The big freighter loomed so large out of the mist that March knew they might crash. The freighter had just sighted them and hadn't even slowed down. So, without another thought he shouted the order, "Rig for crash dive!"

The klaxon blared through the boat below and March knew that men were leaping to their posts, that Gray was struggling out from his bunk or from behind the wardroom table. Would he come up to the bridge? March knew there might not be any bridge—or any conning tower—by the time he could get there, no matter how fast he moved.

He glanced at the deck hatches and breathed a sigh of relief when he saw they were already closed, for the rolling seas were washing over the decks and none of the crew men had wanted to come up for fresh air on a day like this. In a few seconds only the word came back to him, "Boat rigged for crash dive!"

He had already motioned the lookouts down into the hatch, and the control man was securing his gear on the bridge.

"Take her down!" he ordered, as the control man slid down the hatch. He heard the bubbling hiss of air from the main ballast vents, the roar of water as it rushed into the tanks through the huge Kingston valves. With a last glance, he saw in a flash many details on the freighter. Most of all, he saw that it looked tremendous, that it seemed almost on top of him, although he realized that its size in comparison with the half-submerged sub made it look closer than it really was. He saw officers on the bridge shouting orders, and men rushing to man a three-inch gun on the forward deck. Then he slipped below, swung the hatch shut after him and dogged it down before slipping on down into the control room.

The Big Freighter Came Head On

The Diesels had stopped their roar, and the electric motors were whining a high-pitched song as they drove the boat with all their power. He glanced at the "Christmas Tree" and smiled to see nothing but green lights. Every opening, every vent, was closed and the boat was tight. The inclinometer showed them close to a fifteen degree angle of dive, the maximum that was safe before the acid in the batteries would spill out.

Only then did he notice Larry Gray and Ray Corvin and McFee standing motionless, tense, in the middle of the control room. They were listening, waiting. And March listened and waited too, expecting any moment the rending, tearing sound of a steel bow crashing through their superstructure, through their outer hull, through the inner pressure hull—and then, the deluge as the ocean poured in upon them.

One second—two seconds—three seconds—four seconds passed, and then March relaxed.

"All right now," he said. "She'd have hit now if she were going to. She was that close."

He saw a few of the men relax a bit and begin to breathe again. But most of them remained silent and tense. They did not share his confidence, or have confidence in his judgment. He glanced at the depth gauge and saw it at fifty-five feet. Well—it all depended on how much water that freighter was drawing. Maybe it would still knock a few pieces off the conning tower, at least.

But then he heard the soundman say, "Propellers passing over."

"How close?" Gray asked sharply.

"Just about kissing us," came the answer. "But passing over—past now."

Then everyone *did* relax. The crewmen began to talk a bit among themselves. Scotty looked at March and grinned, wiping a hand over his brow as if to brush away the sweat of fear, and then clasped both hands in a congratulatory signal. March just nodded.

"Nice work, Anson," Gray said quietly. "That was a close one. Let's have a cup of coffee. You probably need it."

They turned toward the wardroom together, and March felt the eyes of all crewmen on him.

"Steady at a hundred feet," the Skipper ordered before leaving the control room, "and keep on course."

"Steady at one hundred," came back the order. "Yes, sir."

Then the officers went into the wardroom and sat down just as Stan appeared at the door.

"What in blazes happened?" he asked.

"We just about got run down, that's all," the Skipper smiled. "Not an uncommon occurrence in submarining, Bigelow. Your friend Anson here took us down in a big hurry."

"Were *you* on the bridge, March?" Stan asked.

"Yes, if you'd known that," March laughed, "you would have been twice as scared, wouldn't you?"

"Wow, we went down in a big hurry, all right," Stan said. "Did you have to—to miss it?"

"Guess so," March said. "Anyway, they were unlimbering a gun the last thing I saw and would've been shooting at us if we'd still been in sight."

"Yes, you did the right thing, all right," Gray said. "And without much time to think about it."

"But the crew was marvelous," March said. "I got the call back that the ship was rigged almost before I got the order out of my mouth. It's a good feeling to know a crew can act like that, isn't it, Gray? Especially when a third of it is brand new."

"Yes, mighty satisfying," Larry agreed. "And just as satisfying to know the same thing about your new officers. I'm going to feel pretty confident when we suddenly have six Jap destroyers pouncing on us all of a sudden."

"Say, I just thought of something," Corvin said. "Those poor guys in that freighter are probably still looking frantically for signs of a periscope and sitting there biting their nails waiting for a torpedo to blast them to kingdom come."

Gray looked at his watch. "They're just about getting over that by now," he said. "They're just concluding that we *are* an American sub and not a German. And they're thanking their lucky stars."

"Just like us," McFee added.

In a few minutes the Skipper went out and ordered the sub up to periscope depth, had the 'scope run up and took a look around.

"Not a thing in sight," he announced. "Down 'scope."

As the big shaft slid down into its well in the deck, the Skipper ordered the ship to surface once again, and up she came. Gray was the first man up on the bridge, and the other officers quickly followed him. Lookouts and controlmen took their posts, and the *Kamongo* went steadily ahead on her course.

Corvin took over the watch on the bridge and in a little while the others went below. The crew had settled down and once more everything was serene and quiet.

More days went by, but without the excitement of even a sight of ship or plane. After they had passed into the Caribbean Sea, the Skipper ordered them to hold up for two hours before proceeding.

"We're a bit ahead of schedule," he explained, "because of the extra speed we made on the surface. Coming into Panama, we've got to surface and run exactly on schedule and on course. Patrol craft and planes are expecting us and they'll bomb us out of sight if we're five minutes off schedule or two degrees off course."

When they resumed speed, on the surface, March checked the boat's position regularly to make sure of their course. The first time a big Martin PBM-1 shot out of a cloud ahead of them, March felt his throat grow dry. If they were *not* exactly where they should be at that moment, he knew what would happen to a beautiful new sub and about sixty-four good men of Uncle Sam's Navy.

But the patrol plane just circled low overhead, gunned its motors and flew away. He knew that its radio reported the sub's position to other patrol craft, and that they would be checked up on regularly.

Two other planes came over for a look on their way in toward the Canal, and for the last twenty-five miles they were sighted by half a dozen surface ships.

"Are we to go right on through without stopping?" March asked the Skipper.

"Stop long enough to take on the Canal pilot," he replied. "Nothing else."

The Skipper was on the bridge, along with Corvin, as they ran alongside the jetty leading to the first locks. As they tied up at the dock below the locks, Corvin stepped ashore. He came back shortly with a gray-haired man who would pilot them through the Canal. The weather was clear and the sun beat down warmly, so half the crew were lined up on the deck, and all hatches were open. All officers were on the bridge, except McFee, who stayed below in charge. Even Stan left his Diesels long enough to come up for a look at the Canal, for all the submarine's engines were off as they were pulled through the locks by the little donkey engines running on tracks alongside.

The Canal pilot came aboard and climbed to the bridge. Lines were cast, cables attached fore and aft to the donkey engines on both sides, and they began to move forward on the pilot's orders. Ahead March saw the huge steel doors into the first lock. Slowly and steadily the pigboat moved into the chamber, and the great doors swung silently shut behind them.

Then water rushed into the lock and the boat gently moved upward as the surface of the water rose. Soon they were level with the water in the next lock and the gates ahead of them swung back against the walls. They saw, in the lock next to them, a battered destroyer heading the other direction.

"She's been through something, all right," Gray commented. "Going home for repairs."

The crew on the destroyer waved to the men on *Kamongo* and for a time there were shouts back and forth. Then they had moved out of the second lock into Gatun Lake, as the destroyer sank down in its lock toward the level of the ocean.

Sailing through the lake was like a pleasant excursion trip on a lake steamer. The thick jungles were unlike anything most of the men had seen before and they looked about them with curiosity.

Through the locks at Pedro Miguel and then at little Lake Miraflores, and they were once more at sea level—this time at the level of the Pacific.

They dropped the pilot at the edge of the long breakwater and then headed out to sea, looking back at the lights of the city of Panama which were beginning to twinkle in the growing darkness.

"Not much time for sightseeing when you're on submarines," Stan said, as he and March climbed down to the control room.

"Not when there's a war going on, anyway," March said. "We're in the Pacific now, Stan. How does it feel?"

"Just like the Atlantic," Stan said.

"Not to me," March mused. "This is the ocean we're going to do our fighting in. This is the ocean where I've already done a fair amount of battling Japs. But this time, I think I'm going to do a lot better."

CHAPTER ELEVEN

UNDER WAY AGAIN

In San Francisco, Stan and March had two days for a little of the sightseeing they had looked forward to, but they both spent most of their time at other tasks. March passed several hours at a telephone stand trying to get through a call home.

When it finally went through he talked for five minutes with his mother and gave her his San Francisco address. She sounded cheerful and not at all worried, and asked him if he might see Scoot Bailey.

"Scoot's address is San Francisco, too," she said.

"I know," March laughed, "and the address of quite a few thousands of other sailors and soldiers. I think he must have got out of Frisco before this, unless he was held up here for lack of transportation. I might as well try to find out, though."

"Maybe you'll see him out where you're going," his mother said.

"I doubt it very much," March said. "Even though we did have a joke about how my submarine would probably have to save him from the Japs out there."

When he finished talking to his mother, he decided he might as well try to find out if Scoot were still in town. He had probably arrived two or three weeks before. It wasn't likely that he'd still be around, but sometimes men were held up that long.

"If Scoot *were* held up that long," March said to himself, "he'd be just about crazy. I think he'd start swimming to get out to his carrier or plane or base or wherever he'll be."

March spent most of the afternoon trying to find out about Scoot. Each office said it didn't have the information or couldn't give it to him, until he finally reached the right place and learned that Scoot had left San Francisco by plane for his "destination" twelve days before.

He met Stan for dinner, after which they went to a movie. The Skipper had given them leave until a few hours before they were due to sail.

After the movie Stan and March went back to their ship to find that Ray Corvin had suddenly been taken sick. Just as they came up, the ambulance was taking him away to the Naval Hospital.

"Burst appendix, I think," Gray said. "And if that's it, I don't know what we'll do. I'm hoping it's nothing more than an acute indigestion that'll pass in a day or two. But Sallini felt sure it was the appendix and so did the doc that came. That's why they rushed him right off to the hospital."

"Anything we can do?" March asked.

"No, just keep your fingers crossed," Gray said. "Ray's a mighty good man to have aboard a submarine."

"Why, we couldn't go without him, could we?" Stan asked.

"The Navy doesn't wait around for an officer to get over appendicitis," Larry said. "We're scheduled to pull out of here at dawn day after tomorrow morning, and that's when we'll pull out, with or without Ray Corvin."

"What about his family?" March asked. "Didn't he say he lived near here?"

"Sure—about fifty miles away," the Skipper replied. "He had just phoned them before he got this attack. I had to tell them he couldn't come down as he'd planned. I got in touch with the Commandant here and he has sent a car down there for Ray's wife and daughter. They'll see him at the hospital."

In the morning they learned that Corvin's appendix *had* burst and he had been operated on. Larry Gray had spent a good part of the night at the hospital.

"He'll pull through all right," he said wearily. "But it will be weeks before he's up and around. We're really lucky, I guess, that it didn't happen when we were at sea. If it had to happen, it couldn't have timed itself better. In port near a hospital—and not far from Ray's home. He can go there to convalesce."

"What about us?" Stan asked. "It's a shame we can't have him with us. He's a swell guy."

"And a fine officer," Gray said. "He ought to have a command of his own, really. Well, I'm not sure what we'll do. The Navy can probably find us another officer in a hurry if we demand it, though it's not easy to find a good sub man just like that who isn't already occupied."

He shook his head as he turned to his quarters. "I'm not sure just what we'll do," he said, "except that we'll get under way on schedule."

At the door, he stopped. "March, will you and Stan help Mac oversee the loading? I've got to have a little rest."

There wasn't much to come aboard. Ammunition and torpedoes were still intact, so they had to take on only oil and water and food, plus some special medical supplies for use in tropical climates. Stan had ordered a few more spare parts for his engines and motors. With his little repair shop, he felt able then to take care of almost anything that might happen in his department.

It was late that afternoon that the Skipper called March to his quarters.

"Sit down, March," he said. "I've decided what to do about another officer, but I think I ought to talk it over with the rest of you first to see if you agree."

"Whatever you say is all right with the rest of us, Larry," March said. "You know that."

"Perhaps," Larry replied with a smile. "But this involves a little more work for everybody and I want you all to agree that it's best. You see, I think we've got a good crew here—men and officers alike. We get along. We know our business. Getting along together is mighty important in this work, and I don't know how another officer would fit in even if we could get one."

"I know," March agreed. "You can never tell until you've lived in each other's laps for a while, as we have."

"So I want to skip getting—or trying to get—another officer to replace Ray," the Skipper went on. "Plenty of subs this size have operated with four officers and so can we. But we'll have to split up Ray's work."

"Okay with me," March said at once. "What can I take on?"

"That's why I wanted to talk to you alone first," Gray said. "I want *you* to take over Ray's job, really."

"You mean as diving officer," March said, with a thrill.

"Yes, and as executive officer, too," Larry said.

March started to say something, and then he realized exactly what Gray had said. On his first real patrol, he was asked to serve as second in command of a new submarine! It was unbelievable!

"But—Larry," he said. "Do you think I can handle it?"

"If *you* think so," the Skipper said with a smile, "then I think you can, too. I think you can handle just about anything on a submarine that you want to handle."

"What about McFee?" March asked. "He's been out before—been with you before. He's had more experience."

"No—not McFee," Larry said. "Mac's a wonder at his job, and he could take over just about any other submarine job in an emergency. But—well, Mac knows this as well as I do—he's just not quite enough of an executive to handle this. I know that he just wouldn't want the job. He doesn't like to tell people what to do. He wouldn't like to be a general manager, and that's what an executive officer is, really."

"Well, you know him well," March said, "but won't he feel a little funny about having a raw recruit, so to speak, put over him?"

"Not Mac," Larry answered. "He's not like that. Anyway, how about it?"

"Well—I'm mighty pleased that you've got enough confidence in me to ask me," March said. "And I surely ought to have as much confidence in myself as someone else has. Okay, Skipper, you're on."

"Swell, March," Gray said with a broad smile. "I don't feel so bad about not having Ray now. We're going to do a job in *Kamongo*."

"I just hope I can navigate and dive and exec," March said, "all at the same time."

"I Want You to Take Over Ray's Job!"

"Well, I never did think a navigating officer had enough to do just navigating," Gray said, laughing. "And you're never busy navigating when you have to dive. As for being an exec, a well-run sub with a good crew doesn't need much general managing, you'll find. Anyway, Mac and Stan will help you out in that department if you need any help. And don't forget that there is, after all, still a Skipper on the boat who ought to do a little work once in a while."

Later, in the wardroom with Stan and Mac, Larry told them all the new setup, and March was happy to see how obviously pleased with the arrangement McFee and Stan were.

"I was worried," McFee said. "I was afraid you'd get another officer and he'd turn out to be a guy who pulled puns or was a bridge fiend or something terrible like that. And we wouldn't have time to find it out before we got under way, so we'd have to drown him at sea."

"Well, I'd better go report to the Commandant and tell him the arrangement," Larry said. "The Navy likes to know about these things, even if they do leave most decisions up to a ship's captain."

After Gray left, March stepped into the control room. Scotty rushed up to him and shook his hand vigorously.

"Congratulations, Lieutenant!" the radioman cried. "Gee, it's swell!"

"Thanks, Scotty," March grinned. "But how on earth did the crew ever learn this so fast?"

"Didn't you ever hear that the crew always knows the important things before the officers on a sub?" Scott said with a laugh.

"It must be, it must be," March replied, with a shake of his head.

When Larry Gray returned from seeing the Commandant, March thought he noticed a sparkle in his eyes and a smile on his face that he was trying not to show.

"What happened?" he asked.

"Oh, nothing," Larry replied, looking a little embarrassed. "I just reported and he said okay. Everything set for dawn?"

"Everything set," March replied.

"Oh, by the way," Larry said, as if trying to change the subject. "You move your stuff into Ray's quarters. Then you and Stan can both have a little more room to move around in."

"Okay, Skipper," March answered. "Could we see Ray before we leave?"

"No, no more visitors," Larry said. "His family is there, and they let me see him for a minute to say goodbye and good luck from all of us. He's feeling pretty lousy with drainage tubes in him, and worse than that because he can't go along with us. If they'd let him, he'd try to get up and come along right now. He says he could recuperate faster in a sub, anyway, than on dry land. He highly approved of your appointment, by the way."

It was an hour later that March learned the reason for the Skipper's hidden smile and slightly embarrassed look. Noticing a new large sheet of paper on the bulletin board in the crew's quarters he paused to look at it.

"Scuttlebutt Special!!!!" it read. "The brass hats have seen the light at last and promoted our Old Man to Lieutenant Commander! It's about time!"

March walked quickly back to the wardroom where he found Larry Gray and McFee smoking and talking.

"Well, I was told that the crew knew everything important before the officers," he said. "But why did you want to keep it secret?"

Larry almost blushed.

"Oh, so you found out?"

"It's on the bulletin board!" March exclaimed.

"Oh, my golly! These sub crews!" Larry exclaimed. "They can even read your thoughts!"

"Say, what's all this about?" Mac cried. "Let me in on it!"

"Go read it for yourself," March said. "The Skipper made me find it out the hard way."

As Mac squeezed out from behind the little table and hurried down the companionway, March put out his hand and shook Larry's.

"Congratulations, Skipper," he said.

"Thanks, March," Gray said. "Some of the crew on shore liberty must've run into it up at headquarters somehow. They don't miss a thing."

They not only missed nothing, but they did not miss a chance to do something about it. After mess a delegation from the crew appeared and asked for an audience with the Skipper. He sensed what was coming and met them in the control room.

Pete Kalinsky, Chief Petty Officer in the torpedo room, was the spokesman.

"Lieutenant Commander Gray, sir," he said. "Your crew is very happy to see you gettin' up where you belong, though they've got to come through a few more times before it's okay with us. We knew you wouldn't bother about such things, but the *Kamongo's* captain ought to do himself proud, so on behalf of the crew I give you these."

He coughed, acted as if he were about to add something else, then said "Sir," lamely, and backed up.

Larry took the small packages Pete had handed him and undid them with fingers that shook slightly. First came a set of three gold stripes, two wide and one narrow, for his blue uniform. Then the same in black for his work uniform. Then shoulder insignia and finally two gold oak-leaves for pinning on his shirt collars.

March, who stood behind Larry, felt a lump in his throat. He knew how Larry must be feeling and wondered how he could keep the tears out of his eyes. There was a long silence, and March knew that Larry was waiting for his voice to get under control before he spoke. Everyone was looking at him as he fingered the marks of his new rank which had been presented to him by his crew. Not only had they got the news almost as soon as it had happened, but somebody had taken up a collection and rushed downtown, during his last hours of shore leave, to buy these things for him.

"You know, men," Larry spoke quietly, "it's naturally very pleasant to get a promotion. But when you're about to set out in a pigboat to sink as many Jap ships as possible, it doesn't seem very important. And certainly gold braid and pretty gold leaves aren't important at all. But I'll tell you what really *is* important, what really *does* count for a lot when you're about to get under way for enemy waters. That is the knowledge that I have a crew like mine! I've got a crew that is proud of its boat, proud of its Skipper, proud of itself. A crew that'll do something—like this—like what you've just done—well, it just can't be licked, that's all."

CHAPTER TWELVE

VISIT TO WAKE ISLAND

They went all the way to Pearl Harbor on the surface. They had beautiful clear weather each day. Jap ships and subs and planes had been cleared from the entire area so effectively that American submarines did not need to fear being mistaken by their own patrols for Jap subs. They made good time, and the crew and officers alike were happy, in the highest of spirits.

March laughed, one day, as he looked down from the bridge and saw clothes drying on the line, put there by the crew who took the first opportunity to give their things a good sunning.

"This doesn't look much like war," he mused. "Very domestic scene, really. And some of the men have been on deck enough to get a little sunburn. Not the usual picture of the submariner, pale and dehydrated, after his long days beneath the waters of the deep."

But he knew there would be plenty of that life ahead of them. He was happy that this part of the trip was so pleasant. It meant a lot to the crew, who were inclined sometimes to be superstitious, despite all protestations to the contrary. They felt that everything would go well with them since the start of their real patrol had been so auspicious.

The Skipper had opened his orders twelve hours out from San Francisco. They were no great surprise to anyone. They were to go by way of Pearl Harbor to a submarine base in the southwest Pacific, a tiny island where a sub tender nursed its brood of pigboats, fed them oil and torpedoes and supplies before sending them out to break up the Jap shipping lines.

The stop at Pearl Harbor was short, but March enjoyed it, remembering when he and Scoot had left the *Plymouth* there, heading back for the United States and their training in submarines and airplanes. Much to his surprise there was a letter for him. He had not thought anyone would have a chance to write since learning his San Francisco address. The envelope, a plain one with a typed address, gave him no clue:

It was from Scoot! Dated three weeks before, it said, "In case you come this way you'll get this. I'm on the carrier *Bunker Hill* heading for where all of us head when we get out here. Don't forget to come and save me from those Japs when I holler for you!"

That was all, but it was good. It was just like Scoot and it made March feel fine to read it and to picture again his old friend. He showed the note to Larry when he went back to *Kamongo*, and told him about Scoot Bailey.

"Sounds like a swell guy," Larry said. "Why couldn't he have gone into submarines, too?"

"No—he's swell, but he's not right for pigboats," March said. "Too much of an individualist. He'll take orders fine, do a swell job, but he's best when he's on his own. Flying a fighter plane off a carrier is just exactly right for Scoot."

"Well, you never can tell—maybe we'll run into him," Larry said. "Stranger things have happened in wartime."

They sailed from Pearl Harbor looking for action, but several days went by without a sign of ship or plane of any kind.

"We've got to run into something," Larry said one day in the wardroom. "I'd hate to show up at the base with all my torpedoes intact, without a single Jap ship accounted for. Why, we're going through about nine hundred miles of enemy waters and we've got to get something on the way."

"The boys out here have been scaring them into their ratholes," McFee said. "They don't come out any more than they have to."

"But that's the point," Larry said. "They've got to come out sometime. They've got garrisons on a lot of these islands, and garrisons need to be supplied."

"Well, they're just letting the garrisons on lots of those islands starve to death," Stan said.

"Sure, in the Marshalls and a few other places where we've got 'em surrounded," the Skipper said. "But they're still supplying and reinforcing plenty of places around these parts. They lose some ships every day. I just want them to lose a couple to us, as we're passing by on our way to more important things."

"What about Wake Island?" March asked.

"Yes, they're still supplying Wake," Larry said. "We're not too far away from it any more, but we haven't got it really cut off. But our course isn't very close to Wake."

"Couldn't we just edge over that way and have a look?" March asked.

"Well, now, maybe we could," Larry said. "Nobody told us just what course to follow out here. When we get a bit further we've got to run submerged most of the time anyway. We just laid down the straightest route to our destination. But a little detour wouldn't do any harm. Lieutenant Anson, carry us over near Wake."

With a smile, March left the wardroom and went to the navigating desk. There he plotted the course for Wake Island, went up on the conning tower for a shot of the sun to check his course, and gave the new course to the helmsman. Then he went back to the wardroom.

"About six hundred Army-Navy time, courtesy of Whoozis watches," he announced, "we shall sight Wake Island."

"Hm, works out very nicely," Larry said. "Tomorrow morning just after dawn. We can travel on the surface all night and submerge just before the approach."

Everyone was up and about early the next morning, even those who had been on watch during the night. Breakfast was over and officers and men were at their stations before dawn.

"We may get nothing, of course," Larry said. "We mustn't get our hopes up."

"Okay, Skipper," McFee said. "We're just dropping by for a look and if anything's there we'll try to take care of it."

"Rig ship for diving," the Skipper said, and the word was passed throughout the boat. One by one the departments reported back to March that everything was ready. The long slim boat slid under the water, the whine of the electric motors replacing the throbbing of the Diesels. As March handled the diving operations, he recalled the days when it had seemed to him such a complicated and difficult task. Now it was a simple straightforward job, especially when carried out by a crew that knew its job.

After about twenty minutes, March turned to Larry. "I think we ought to be able to have a look now," he said.

"Up periscope," Larry said, reaching forward to grab the adjusting handles as they rose into position. He adjusted the eyepiece and looked, focussing with the handles. March saw his mouth open slightly in a whispered exclamation.

"Have a look, March," he said. "I think we've raised something."

March looked and saw the low-lying atolls where the Marines had for so long battled the Japs against great odds. It would do his heart good to kill a few Japs at Wake, entirely apart from the excellence of the idea in general. He located the harbor and then saw two dark blobs in it.

"There's something there, all right," he said. "Can't be sure what they are yet, though."

"Down 'scope," Larry said. "We'll get a little closer and have another look."

There was almost nothing said as the boat moved silently forward under the water, until Larry ordered the periscope up again. Then he exclaimed aloud at what he saw.

"Three of 'em!" he cried. "Looks as if they just got here themselves, probably came in under cover of darkness. Lighters are just tying up to them to unload."

"What are they?" March asked. "Can you make out?"

"One's a troopship," Larry replied, "loaded to the gunwales! The men'll go ashore in the lighters. They haven't even started yet. Must be relief for the garrison—old ones will be going back."

He Adjusted the Eyepiece and Looked

"Oh, no they won't," March said. "Not yet, anyway, because their relief is going to be cut down in number right soon now."

"Here, March, have a look," Larry said. "I think one's a tanker, one an ammunition ship, or a freighter with the supplies."

March stepped to the periscope and looked carefully.

"Tanker and troopship are certain," he said. "Can't be sure about the other, though. How many do you think we can get?"

"Not more than two," Larry said. "They'll get planes after us that fast. We'll have to get away after two, maybe after one. Can't tell until we're in the middle of it. But what about all the reefs around here? Can we get in position to fire?"

"If we're good we can," March said. "Come on, I'll show you. I've been studying the Wake Island chart, and we know it's right."

Larry followed March to the navigation desk, where they both studied the chart of Wake Island.

"We have to go west first," March said. "Then cut back sharply in a hairpin turn—go in about four hundred yards, turn about thirty degrees to starboard without going forward too much, fire and then back away. Backing will be slow, but we can't turn her for a couple of hundred yards. Think we can make it?"

"Deep water out here?" Larry asked, pointing to a point about a mile off shore.

"Plenty deep," March replied.

"Then I think we can do it," Larry said. "Those ships are worth the chance, anyway. If we're slow getting the first one, we'll cut and run."

"Which one first?" March asked.

"The tanker," Larry said. "Most important. Planes can't fly without the gas and oil it carries."

"Not the troopship?"

"No, too many of the men will be able to swim or get ashore some way," Larry said. "We could count on about fifty percent casualties there. But the tanker—that'll be all gone, and maybe set fire to a few other things. Tanker first, then troopship."

The Skipper gave orders to move the boat to the west around the reefs as March had indicated. March stood close by the soundman, who could tell at every instant just how far they were from the rocky shoals that might trap them.

Slowly the boat moved forward and then, when March gave the word, it turned and moved in toward the island.

"I hope I'm right," March said to himself. "There's not very much room here, though if those ships got through, we surely can."

The sound man picked up reefs to the right and then to the left—nothing ahead, and March breathed more deeply. They went forward for a few moments, still moving slowly.

"About now, March?" Larry asked quietly.

"Yes, this ought to be it," March replied. He saw Scotty at the soundman's side, the other crew members standing by their levers and valves. They were all calm and quiet, but with just a touch of excited expectancy in their manner.

The Skipper gave the order for the turn to starboard, for the cutting of motors. Then he called for the periscope. As it rose from its well in the deck he crouched and grabbed it. Then March realized why Larry was a good Skipper. In just about two seconds he had seen everything there was to see. He called out the course settings for the torpedoes, first for two to go into the sides of the tanker, then for two to go into the sides of the transport.

The settings were called back to him, and he called, without a moment's hesitation—"Fire one! Fire two!" He waited a moment, glancing at his watch. "Fire three! Fire four!"

Stepping away from the eyepiece he called, "Down periscope!" and followed it immediately with "Reverse motors!"

As the whine of the motors started and the boat slid backwards in the water, he kept his eyes on his watch, finger in the air as if counting. He lifted his eyes and—thud! The submarine trembled and shook from the explosion of a torpedo against the side of a ship. There was a wild cry throughout the pigboat as the crew whooped with glee, so loud that it almost drowned out the roar of the second torpedo hitting home against the tanker.

Men danced and jigged, but not for a moment did they take their hands from their levers or wheels, or their eyes from the dials they watched.

"You can turn now, Skipper," March said quietly, and Larry gave the order for the ship to turn and dive deep as it cleared the reefs.

The words were not out of his mouth when another roar sent a tremble through the submarine and another shout arose. It was a short roar because the men stopped to listen for the second torpedo that had been sent against the troopship. But nothing came, and it was Larry who broke the silence.

"A miss, men," he said. "Only one got through."

"Well, what can you expect?" Scotty demanded. "After all, the position we were in!"

"Are still in!" Larry exclaimed. "Only a hundred feet! Take her to two-fifty!"

Everybody adjusted his body to the slope of the boat as it slid rapidly down in the water. In a few minutes, they knew, depth charges would be dropped in an attempt to locate them. Certainly planes would be in the air and perhaps fast small boats something like our own PT-boats would be dashing out of the harbor after them.

Larry grabbed the phone from the interphone orderly and spoke into it.

"You heard the blasts," he said, knowing that men all over the boat would hear him. "Two into a Jap tanker. One into a troopship. Second one there was a dud. You can expect some depth charges, but I think we'll be down away from them. Later we'll go up for a look and I'll tell you what we did."

March knew that all the men appreciated that. They were tense and excited and they wanted to know exactly what was going on. Their Skipper didn't keep them waiting long. They were part of this just as much as he was.

They leveled off at two hundred and fifty feet just as they felt the first bumping rattle of a depth charge explosion. But it was far away and hardly bothered them. In two minutes another came a little closer. Everyone gripped the nearest solid support and held on. March said to himself, "You're going through a depth bombing. This was the one thing they couldn't simulate at New London. Well, how do you like it?"

And he answered himself, "It's not so bad."

He looked around at the men in the crew. They held on and they listened, but they did not look frightened. Larry grinned at him.

"Lousy aim they've got," he said. "They're not coming very close."

"What about a little zigzagging?" March asked.

"No, we might zig or zag into something," Larry said. "They obviously haven't located us and are just dropping at random. Also, we're deep enough to be below the explosions. After all, the biggest force of the blow is above the exploding charge. We'll just keep sliding along the way we're going. They'll give up after a while."

The charges exploded regularly, but not for long. Soon they hardly felt a jar when one went off.

"They think we're hanging around back there for a look," Larry said. "They don't know how safe we play. I'm not going back for my look for two hours. So just keep going."

They did keep going, and for two hours. By the time they circled around and came back toward the island there were no more depth charges. About a mile away they surfaced quickly and the Skipper took a quick look. Then the 'scope went down and March ordered another dive.

"Sorry you couldn't have had a look, March," Larry said, "but I didn't—"

He was interrupted by a shaking roar that almost spilled him off his feet. March, who had one hand against the bulkhead, grabbed him.

"As I was saying," Larry went on with a smile, "I didn't want to keep the 'scope up any longer than I had to. They spotted it pretty fast, didn't they?"

Another roar was the answer, followed by another and another, and half a dozen more. They were bad shocks, worse than those they had experienced at first, but the sub had got down fast enough to get away from the worst effects.

"What did you see?" March asked between blasts.

"Listen," Larry said. He took the interphone and gave his news to the whole ship. "Tanker down—only the bow showing, oil-covered water blazing over the entire bay. Total loss for the Nips on that one. Troopship looks half busted in two, but still afloat, though listing badly. No men on her. Plenty of bodies in the water. Lots got ashore, I'm sure, but plenty got burned in the oil trying to make it."

A loud cheer rose through the ship as Larry handed the phone back to the orderly.

"Well, anyway," he said. "It was certainly worth four torpedoes!"

As the *Kamongo* slid down through the dark waters, the depth charges grew less intense. Finally they got away from them entirely, and resumed the course for their southwest Pacific base.

"Don't let that fool you," Larry said, as they sat in the wardroom having a cup of coffee. "There weren't any sound detectors there, so we got away pretty easily. When the destroyers are after you, they *follow* you—and their depth charges are bigger. This was a setup!"

CHAPTER THIRTEEN

SCOOT MEETS TWO ZEROS

Scoot Bailey lounged in the ready room of the aircraft carrier *Bunker Hill* as the big ship plunged through heavy seas at top speed. They had been at sea for some weeks now, in company with a cruiser and three destroyers, heading southwest from Pearl Harbor for scenes of battle. For the last two days the five ships had put on full steam, and everyone aboard knew that something was up.

"Something's cooking up ahead," Scoot said to Turk Bottomley, who sat next to him, legs stretched out on a straightback in front of him.

"Obviously, my friend," Turk said. "Something's been cooking in this part of the world almost all the time lately."

"I thought we'd be heading for the Marshalls and the Carolines," Scoot said, "to get in on the fighting there. But I guess they've got things well in hand in those parts. We're well past them now, and to the south."

"No flying for two days now," Turk said. "That's what's been bothering me. Before we got off once in a while for a look around, anyway. I want to fly, that's all. I won't worry about where. Let the Admirals send me where they want me, but let me fly and fight when I get there—and, if possible, on the way, too."

"Gee, I thought I loved flying," Scoot said, with a laugh, "but I never held a candle to you."

"Yeah, I even resent walkin'," Turk said. "Seems like I should've had wings instead of legs—just for gettin' around short distances. I'd still want that Grumman Hellcat for longer jumps."

"They're sweet ships, all right," Scoot said. "I used to dream of flying a Wildcat—thought there just couldn't be anything better than that. And I still thought so when I finally flew one off the training carrier. She was an old one, but still a Wildcat. Then when I get here on the *Bunker Hill*, I find the brand new F6F's—and Hellcat is the right name. They're what a Wildcat pilot dreams up as impossibly perfect when he thinks about what kind of plane he'll have in Heaven."

"Poetic, now, aren't you, Scoot?" Turk said. "I can't put words together that way, but it sounds nice when you talk about planes. Sometimes, when you get real excited, you almost talk the way I feel."

Suddenly they sat up, as did the four or five others in the large room. Other pilots began to pile into the room followed by most of the big-shot officers on the ship.

"Oh-oh—here it comes!" Scoot said. "Now we'll find out. It looks like a briefing."

There were fighter pilots, the pilots, gunners and observers of torpedo and scout dive bombers, and the squadron leaders of each group, accompanied by the particular vice-admiral in command of the force now racing across the Pacific. This rugged, beetle-browed gentleman lost little time in getting down to business. Addressing the flying officers before him while other officers hung a huge map on the wall behind, he quickly gave them the information they wanted.

"You've all known we've been heading for something as fast as we could get there," he said, in clipped tones. "Now I can tell you, because we've made speed and are not far away. Within a few hours we should contact other carriers and ships going to the same objective. That objective is the Jap Naval base at Truk."

There was a gasp of surprise throughout the room as the Admiral paused for a second.

"There's a mighty fine batch of ships in Truk Harbor," he said, "and, we have reason to believe, not too much protection. Carriers—and there'll be six of them—will go in close enough to launch all planes. Battleships, cruisers, and destroyers will go in closer."

Turk Bottomley was sitting on the edge of his chair, as if he would bound from the room and race to his plane in a second, but the Admiral continued.

"The time is now about 1600. We shall rendezvous with the others of the task force at about 2030. You will take off on a schedule your squadron commanders will give you beginning at 0430, arriving over Truk about dawn—the first wave, that is. All scout and torpedo planes will go to Truk, one-half the fighters will remain as protection with or near the carrier. Your squadron commanders will go over all necessary details with you now. That is all."

The Admiral stalked from the room, and the commanders prepared to go over all details. They launched at once into detailed descriptions of the objective, the schedule of flights.

"If we've figured right," one of them said, "we'll stick around two days, throwing in wave after wave. We must meet our schedule because it ties in precisely with the schedules of the other carriers in the group. We'll not give them a minute to catch their breath. There'll be planes coming at them continuously."

For two hours the briefing session continued. Photographs and maps were shown, man after man asked questions. Finally every flier felt that he knew Truk and its environs as he knew his own home town. Then came the announcement of the fliers who would remain with the carrier instead of going to the attack on Truk and there were groans about the room as men heard their names called.

"One minute," the fighter squadron commander called. "I think the Old Man gave a wrong impression. The names I'm calling won't stay with the carrier both days. They'll stay behind the first day but go on to the attack the second day, while the first group remains with the carrier."

Groans turned to laughter, but Turk Bottomley was furious. He was going out the first day, but he wanted to go out the second day, too. He made his feelings known in no uncertain terms.

"Never mind, Turk," the commander laughed. "You can go up and fly around and around the *Bunker Hill* all day!"

So it was that Turk flew off in the dark morning hours, while Scoot Bailey stayed behind envying those lucky men whose names had been opposite the odd numbers on the list instead of the even. As plane after plane rolled across the heaving deck of the flat-top and roared off into the overcast sky, Scoot muttered under his breath, wishing that each one might have been his.

Dawn came and there was no word. Scoot went up with half a dozen other fighters to keep eyes on the sea, to attack any Japanese craft that came through to get them. But for hours there was no sign of a plane—either of the enemy or of their own.

Then Scoot, just after he had landed again, heard them far away—the roar of many powerful engines. And in a moment he saw the tiny specks that raced so fast they soon became planes circling in mighty sweeps around the carrier. The first one came in as the signalman waved his paddles for a landing. Deck men and the fighter pilots who were not up in the air lined the edge of the deck, and officers crowded the bridge. As the first pilot scrambled from his plane, the deck crew grabbed it, folded its wings, and raced it back to the elevator so the next plane could land.

In a moment the pilot was talking—and in a few minutes he was joined by another, then another and another.

"We caught 'em with their pants down!" the first yelled. "Flatfooted. We caught 'em right on the airfields! They couldn't get off."

"And when the bombers came in," cried the next, "they had a clear field. How those boys dove! Oil tanks blew up! Ships strewn all over the place, clogging up the harbor!"

One after another the pilots told their stories while mechanics checked their engines, filled the tanks with gas, the guns with ammunition. They all told of how the Japs had been taken by surprise, how plane after plane had been wrecked on the field, how torpedo planes and scout-dive bombers came in with little more than scattered antiaircraft fire to get in their way.

"We've hardly lost a plane so far!" one said. "And have we got planes around there! I haven't seen so many planes since I was at Corpus Christi— but these are not trainers. Fighters, torpedo planes, bombers—coming in like flocks of wild geese. Why, I was just as worried trying not to bump into some of our own craft as by any opposition the Japs put up. The Old Man must be mighty happy. Has he got full reports?"

"He's gettin' 'em first-hand right this minute!" the executive officer of the carrier replied. "He's up there himself in a scout, looking over the whole business. And you can bet your bottom dollar he's the happiest man on earth!"

"What was prettiest," another joined in, "was seeing the planes from the other carriers coming in. From every direction! We were in the first wave, and just as we pulled up and away, there they came—wave number two from the northeast, and a little farther away wave number three from the southeast. You had to hurry and do your job so you could get out of the way of the next batch coming along."

"Where's Turk Bottomley?" Scoot asked. "Did any of you see him?"

"I saw him circling around for another go at one of the airfields," a torpedo-plane pilot said. "At least I think it was Turk's Hellcat I saw. He was joining up with the second wave and going in again."

"He ought to be back by now," someone said. "All the other fighters are in—except Tommy Mixler. I saw him go down in the harbor. Ack-ack."

There was a moment's silence at this unwanted mention of a casualty, of a friend they'd see no more, and then—as if they were forcibly clearing their minds of any such thoughts—the pilots went on chattering again. Their planes were almost ready for them to take off again when they all saw a lone fighter circling the ship. Zooming his engine and doing a beautiful wing-over turn, the pilot brought his plane around into the wind for a landing on the heaving deck of the carrier.

"That's Turk, all right," Scoot said. "Home from the wars."

And it was Turk, almost out of gas and completely out of ammunition. He had stayed around as long as he could, and now he wanted to be off again within five minutes. As soon as his plane was shoved out of the way where it could be checked and get its new supplies of gas and ammunition, the fighters who had come in earlier began to take off again. They were off on schedule, going in for their second attack on Japan's Pearl Harbor of the Pacific!

All day long it went on, with Scoot and the others staying aloft, on the alert for the Jap planes that would surely come through to attack them. No matter how great the surprise, some planes would get off the airfields at Truk and others would race in from other Jap strongholds. They would go for the carriers first, of course, for the flat-tops were the big prizes. With the base ship gone, the planes would be lost without a "home" to return to.

Some Fighters Stayed With the Carrier

But Scoot searched in vain through the skies as the afternoon turned to evening. The *Bunker Hill's* own planes came back for the last time but still no Japs appeared. Scoot was raging—all day long without a crack at a Jap! And they were right in the heart of what the Nips considered their private ocean!

"Is there anything left of Truk for us to get?" he asked that night. "Didn't everything get blasted off the map?"

"There'll be plenty left for everybody," the squadron commander replied. "We've got half the ships in the harbor and we'll get most of the rest tomorrow. Some of them scattered and ran but the boys from the carriers to the north are catching them. There are emergency airfields around that will be in use tomorrow, and you can be sure that there'll be planes from other Jap garrisons in this area. You boys will have a fight on your hands tomorrow all right."

"We'd better have!" Scoot exclaimed. "Imagine! Not a lousy Jap showed up today!"

It was with grim anger that Scoot took off the next morning, reveling in the almost unlimited power of his Hellcat as it roared up into the blue skies and circled, heading for Truk. Scoot was in the squadron leader's group, and their objective was the big airfield south of the city. The Japs would have been working on it all night, despite constant attacks by the bombers, and they'd have at least one landing strip in shape for their planes to get off. The fighters were to strafe the field, then go up as protective cover for the dive bombers. These would be coming into the harbor right after them, to get the rest of the ships that still lay there.

Roaring low over the choppy waters of the Pacific, the speedy planes raced toward the tiny group of islands that the Japs had made into a great naval fortress, a fortress that was being knocked to pieces by American planes.

As they approached the island, Scoot saw ahead several American ships—two cruisers and half a dozen destroyers.

"They're doing it, boys," his squadron leader's voice came over the radio. "The surface ships are moving in close to shell the island!"

Scoot almost laughed in happiness. It was daring enough for American carriers to penetrate supposedly Japanese waters and give a pasting to their impregnable fort. Carriers could stay a couple of hundred miles out while their planes flew in to the attack. And they were fast ships which could get away in a hurry if they needed to. But here were the big-gun ships moving to within fifteen or twenty miles to shell the island. And the Jap Navy was either hiding or running away—in its own back yard!

The fighter planes gunned their engines in greeting as they passed the American ships, and Scoot could see the crews waving and laughing happily on the decks of the ships.

"They'll start their shelling just about the time the dive bombers finish the first part of their job," Scoot guessed. "And when they've pounded away a couple of hours the bombers will come back in again for another attack."

Up ahead lay the island. At better than three hundred miles an hour the huge flight of fighters went over the shore, heading straight for the airfield. They paid no attention to the twenty or thirty Jap fighters high above them, did not even notice the bursts, of ack-ack shells that puffed around and ahead of them. They were too low and traveling too fast for ack-ack to be very effective or accurate—and as for those Zeros, the American planes would take care of them in just a few minutes.

Scoot saw the airfield up ahead, saw Jap planes on the runways ready to take off. And the next minute he was roaring over the field, not thirty feet above the runway, watching the Jap ground crews running for cover, seeing a few firing rifles futilely into the air at the speeding planes. He pressed the machine-gun button and felt the slight backward push to the plane as the battery of fifty caliber machine guns poured out its converging fire of destruction. Jap after Jap, fleeing toward the hangars, was cut down in his tracks. Scoot concentrated a terrific burst of fire on the plane directly ahead of him, saw a flash as it caught fire, then pulled up and away with a shout that could have been heard half a mile away had not the air been filled with the roar of powerful engines.

He circled and came back over the field the other way, this time dipping to pour a hail of lead into the open doors of a hangar.

"How did the other boys happen to leave that one standing?" Scoot wondered. "The others are all down in ruins." It was not easy to demolish a big hangar with a fighting plane, so Scoot left that for the bombers, knowing that he had taken care of a few Japs huddling inside the building and had put forty or fifty holes in the plane standing near the front.

After one more sweep over the field, he pointed his Hellcat's nose at the sun and climbed. But there was something up there on the sun, he thought, looking intently. Sunspots? What a funny thing to think of at a moment like this. He'd hardly be noticing sunspots—but he *would* almost instinctively notice Jap Zeros when they were diving at him out of the sun.

"That's what they are!" Scoot exclaimed. "But they made one big mistake. They thought we were going to strafe the field a couple more times and they'd come down on us out of the sun while we were busy doing it. I'll bet they're confused now, seeing us coming right up at them head-on."

The first groups of the fighter squadrons were all aiming for the clouds after their attack on the field, while the next groups were carrying on the strafing job. And Scoot knew, too, that two groups were high in the air, serving as cover for just such a Jap attack.

"Those Nips may not know it," he muttered to himself, "but I'll bet there's a flock of Hellcats coming out of the sun right behind 'em."

The Zeros were larger now, growing larger every minute as they dived down at the formations of American planes trying to climb away from the field. It looked as if all the planes were determined to crash head-on into each other at the greatest possible speed.

Scoot heard a short command come over the radio from his squadron leader. He grinned.

"Just what I thought he'd do," he told himself, and then shoved the stick hard to the right, as he pulled back on the throttle. The American group split, half going to the right, half to the left, in a maneuver so sudden and sharp that the Japs in their Zeros could hardly believe their eyes at seeing planes which had been almost in their gunsights disappear so quickly. They still thought that their lightly armored Zeros were the most highly maneuverable planes in the world. They'd not had much experience yet with the new Hellcats.

Scoot's wing tipped sharply, and the craft seemed to stall. Then, giving her the gun again, he flipped completely over. He knew that the Japs, in that part of a second, would have roared past the spot he had just been in and now the American planes could chase *them* on down toward the field, coming in from the side and rear.

"There they are!" Scoot cried. "Just about set up in position!"

The first Jap planes were pulling up desperately from their dive, attempting to get back in position to meet the attack of the Americans. Scoot picked the leading Jap plane, got it in his sights and roared up on it from a little below. He held his fire, held it a fraction of a second longer, then pushed the fire-control button with a vicious jab that almost drove it out of its socket.

Black smoke crept back from the Zero, then flame which fast grew into a huge sheet of fire enveloping the entire craft. It slowed, seemed to stagger a moment in the air. Losing power at once because of its climbing position, it twisted and turned.

As Scoot pulled up and away, he kept his eye on the blazing Zero as it fell—at first lazily, then faster and faster—toward the ground.

"Is it going to—Yes, by golly!" Scoot cried as the flaming plane crashed into the huge hangar still standing at the edge of the Jap field below. There was a roar of fire, a great cloud of black smoke and Scoot threw back his head and laughed loud and long.

"Who said a fighter couldn't take care of a hangar?" he demanded. "Why did I think I had to leave it for the bombers? Boy, oh boy, is that good?"

"That's puttin' 'em in the right pocket, Scoot!" It was the voice of his squadron leader over the radio. "But watch out behind you! A little sneak attack coming!"

Yes, there were two Japs coming in on him. Now where did they come from, Scoot wondered. But he didn't spend much time on that question for he had other things to do. If these Japs weren't familiar enough with what the new Hellcats could do he'd show 'em. So, instead of diving to get away, as he knew they expected, he put his fighter into a steep climb that pulled him up toward the clouds as if a giant hand had reached down and grabbed him.

That took the first Jap by surprise, as Scoot hoped, but the second had just enough time to meet the maneuver. As Scoot closed in on the first, he knew that the second was coming in behind him. He concentrated on one thing at a time. Maybe, he thought, he could take care of the first one fast and get away quickly enough. With a roar of speed, he brought the first Jap into range, opened fire, saw smoke, and waited no longer. He plunged into a diving turn, looked back over his shoulder and saw the second Jap ship already plunging earthward in a cloud of smoke.

"Who did that?" Scoot demanded, almost to himself.

"I did, my friend!" It was Turk Bottomley's voice.

"What are you doing here?" Scoot demanded.

"No Jap planes showed up at the carrier," Scoot said, "so the Old Man let a few of us come over to have some fun. I just got here."

"And just in time, lad," Scoot said. "Thanks."

"Don't mention it," Turk laughed. "The pleasure was all mine."

So that is how Scoot managed to paint two little Jap flags on the side of his plane the next day, as the *Bunker Hill* steamed westward, away from a smoking and flaming Truk.

"That's something like it!" Scoot exclaimed to himself. "I'll bet poor old March isn't having any fun like this, cooped up in that stuffy submarine."

It was at that moment that March was listening with pleasure to the explosion of the *Kamongo's* torpedoes against the sides of a Jap tanker at Wake Island.

CHAPTER FOURTEEN

CRASH LANDING

Kamongo was ranged with fourteen other submarines alongside the tender *David* at the little island base in the southwest Pacific. The crossing after the sinking at Wake Island had been uneventful, since they had run submerged most of the time during daylight hours. Always on the lookout for enemy ships, officers and crew alike had been disappointed to run into nothing but an American task force, consisting of a carrier, a cruiser, and three destroyers racing north at full speed.

March had tried to make out the name of the carrier, and he would have been delighted to know it was the *Bunker Hill* carrying Scoot and his companions from their Truk attack to a small action against another Jap-held island farther north. But even American subs submerged and ran deep and quiet when American ships were near by. The destroyers would have started to toss depth charges like snowflakes if they had sighted a periscope of any kind.

At the sub base, all pigboat Skippers and their seconds were at a meeting aboard the tender. Captain Milbank, the Intelligence Officer, was speaking to them.

"You've all heard about the blasting of Truk," he said. "Now, it's certain that the Japs will try to reinforce that important post as quickly and as fully as possible. In fact, word has reached us through the Chinese that a large convoy has already left Japan for Truk, with troops, oil and gasoline, ammunition, more antiaircraft guns, food and supplies, and with almost every deck covered with Zeros. They've got to replace what we knocked out there and, even further, increase their defending force. They know we'll hit it again."

He looked around the room at the quiet, serious faces of the men who listened intently.

"You may also know," he went on, "that we have found Chinese Intelligence to be very reliable. It's amazing how they get word through the Jap lines so quickly and efficiently. Well—the Chinese report that there's something special about this convoy for Truk. They weren't able to learn exactly what it is, but they believe it is in the route to be followed. The Nips know our submarines are roaming the seas out here and will be on the lookout especially for this convoy. Having knocked Truk half out, we want to keep it in that condition. It's you men—with some help, I must confess, from the air service—who will do that job."

There were smiles in the room as the Captain, joking, grudgingly recognized the usefulness of the flying sailors. Then he continued:

"Our patrol planes are ranging over the ocean on the lookout for the convoy, of course, but their distances are limited and it's a mighty big ocean to cover. So, for a while, our submarines must also act as scouts. Later we can get together and sink the ships, but first we have to act as a team to find them.

"We're all going to leave here at the same time, and fan out to cover the main routes from Japan to Truk. And we want to catch them as far from Truk as possible. The earlier we can find them, the more subs and planes we'll have time to get to the attack so we can wipe the whole thing out."

The Captain turned to a chart behind him on the wall.

"Later I shall go over with you the routes to be followed by each submarine," he said. "If and when any one of you sights the convoy he is *not* to radio that information. The Japs would certainly pick up that broadcast. They'd know we had discovered them and they'd be ready for us. We want the attack to come by surprise. So we have arranged certain spots for each of you to arrive at on certain days and at specific hours. A patrol plane will visit each of those spots, clearly marked so that you will not mistake it for an enemy plane. He will land on the water and pick up any information you may have. This same procedure is to be followed twenty-four hours later at another spot further away.

"If by that time not one of you has found the convoy, you are to go your own ways, looking for whatever you can find on this patrol. And by that time, if you find anything like the big convoy, the only thing to do will be to surface and radio us so we can all close in for the kill. We'll lose the element of surprise but we'll get them, anyway."

Next, the Intelligence Officer went over the details of routes and rendezvous spots for each submarine. March saw at once that *Kamongo* was taking a westerly course from their base, then heading northwest. It seemed to him that this should be one of the most likely routes for a convoy to take from Japan to Truk, and he was pleased.

Then Larry Gray asked a question of the Intelligence Officer.

"Those rendezvous spots," he said. "They appear to be in open sea, but I know there are little atolls all over the place. Are they near such islands?"

"No, they are not," the Captain said. "Purposely. The Japs have little garrisons on a great many of those tiny islands that look no more than bumps on the sea. Some of them have radios. If they saw the contact of an American sub and an American patrol plane so far from our bases, they'd report it.

That wouldn't tell the Japs much, but the less they know the better we like it, no matter how unimportant it may seem. No, the meeting places are in open water. The navigators have a little work to do on this patrol."

Larry glanced at March and smiled. March knew it wasn't the easiest thing in the world to find one exact spot in the middle of a big ocean by dead reckoning.

After going over all details of the complicated plan thoroughly, the skipper and their execs returned to their own submarines to see that everything was ready for getting under way. Fuel and supplies and torpedoes had been loaded into all the pigboats and there remained only a final check before they could depart.

In the night they slipped away from their tender one by one and, traveling on the surface under the protection of night, they headed out to sea silently, on the alert, eagerly looking forward to the task ahead. The crew of each pigboat felt that *they* would be the ones to find the convoy, the first to go in for the attack.

But on the second day not a sign of the convoy had been seen by any of the submarines.

"Must be coming more slowly than we thought," Larry suggested. "We'll catch up with it before the next patrol stop."

At the time Larry spoke they were on the surface in the late afternoon, watching the big American flying boat slide down out of the clouds and circle above them. March had felt a thrill of satisfaction when he saw it, knowing that it meant he had found his particular spot in the wide Pacific, but Larry just seemed to take it for granted that his navigator would have brought them where they were supposed to be, no matter how difficult the job.

They gave their negative report to the patrol, learned that no other pigboat contacted had had better luck, then submerged as the flying boat took off from the choppy waters.

They ran submerged at periscope depth for two hours until darkness began to fall, with one of the officers having his eye glued to the little rubber piece on the 'scope every minute. Then they surfaced and went steadily forward on their prescribed course. Two officers and three lookouts stayed constantly on the bridge, and the sound detector man below concentrated on his listening as never before. It might well be that he could pick up the sound of a convoy's propellers long before the lookouts would sight anything, especially on a moonless night.

But dawn came and found them with nothing to report.

"You'd think there wasn't even a war going on out here!" McFee complained. "Don't the Nips have *any* ships in these waters?"

"Not in the waters we've been sailing on, anyway," Stan Bigelow replied. "I feel cross-eyed from looking so hard for the last four hours."

The bright sun sent them under the water again, but only to periscope depth so that a constant lookout could be maintained. Still—late afternoon found them filled with discouragement, waiting for the patrol plane. The patrol had found nothing.

"Maybe one of the others—" March suggested, but Larry shook his head.

"I can't believe it," he said. "I think we're in the best spot. We're furthest west of the whole bunch. That's certainly the most likely route for the convoy, keeping as close to the Philippines, to land protection, as possible. If they were attacked they'd have support from land-based planes there for quite a while. If anything, I think they may even be further west than our route."

March and Larry talked as they stood on the bridge waiting for their patrol plane to come out of the west. Suddenly the lookout shouted, "Plane coming out of the sun!"

"Can't be ours!" Larry shouted. "Rig for dive, March."

As March barked out the orders to take the ship down, the lookout reported that the plane was a two-motored flying boat.

"Must be a Jap all right," Larry said. They all knew that their own plane was four-motored, one of the longest-ranged flying boats in the world.

A Two-Motored Flying Boat Came at Them

In two minutes March had slid down the hatch, to be followed by Larry, who dogged the hatch cover tight.

"Take her down to a hundred and fifty," he said.

Kamongo turned her nose down and slid forward. As they leveled off at a hundred and fifty they heard the roar and felt the jar of a depth charge explosion. But it was not close and it went off far above them. Then came another, a little closer but still threatening no danger to the sub.

"Not full-size charges," Larry said. "We're all right at a hundred and fifty. We'll just wait him out. He can't be carrying very many depth charges in that job of his. But hold on—he'll probably get a little closer."

They all held on, but nothing happened. Not another charge went off. March looked questioningly at Larry.

"Don't know," Larry said. "Maybe he's gone on. More likely he's playing possum, hoping we'll think he's gone and will come up for a look. That's when he'd get us."

"Better stay down for a while," March said.

"Yes, he can't fly around up there in a circle forever," Larry said. "We'll go up in an hour."

"What about meeting our patrol plane?" March asked.

"I'm afraid we'll miss him," Larry said. "Can't take a chance on going up now. He might hang around for a while, of course, if the Jap has gone."

"He could take care of that Jap in a minute," McFee said.

"Say, maybe that's what happened," March suggested.

"Perhaps," said Larry. "Maybe our plane came and drove off the Jap. But we can't be sure. I'm not going to risk a sub and sixty men just to find out."

Then the sound man turned excitedly.

"I hear something, sir," he said. "Something in Morse—sounds like a hammer tapping against metal. I'll have it in a minute."

They waited impatiently as the sound man took down the message. Then he handed it to Larry.

"*Kamongo*," it said. "Jap went home. Come on up."

Larry grinned. "It's okay," he said. "The Jap wouldn't have known we were *Kamongo*. It's our plane. Take her up."

When the ship surfaced and Larry scrambled through the hatch on to the bridge he saw the big American flying boat resting on the water not a quarter of a mile away. It taxied over beside the submarine as March and Mac joined Larry on the bridge.

"I thought you'd get that hammer-on-the-hull message," the plane's pilot called with a smile. "Nippo just took one look at me coming and decided he had a date west of here in a big hurry."

Larry passed on his report of not having sighted the big Jap convoy and learned that no other submarine had found it either.

"Well, you're on your own now," the pilot said. "Go get 'em and good luck."

They waved as the plane turned and roared over the water, lifted in the air and circled to the east with a last dip of its wings.

"Now where do we go from here?" March asked.

"We'll head west," Larry said. "After that Jap plane. Let's get going. I'm going to find that convoy!"

Meanwhile, the Jap plane heading west had sighted something else. Its pilot was angry at having been driven away from an American submarine just when it was about to blow the hated pigboat to its ancestors. And there ahead of him—to make up for that loss—was a lone American fighter plane. He grinned happily.

"American plane," he said to his co-pilot. "We get him."

The co-pilot looked worried. "American fighter too fast for slow flying boat. Maybe he get us!"

But the pilot was angry and not to be argued with. "No, we get American fighter!"

It was obvious that the American had seen them, but the plane did not put on a sudden burst of speed, did not maneuver quickly to get into position for the attack.

The co-pilot grinned. "American plane damaged," he said. "American plane cannot fly fast!"

"Now will you question what I say?" demanded the pilot. "I said we get American plane. Our gods damage plane so we *can* get it."

Scoot Bailey looked at the approaching Jap bomber and frowned. Here was a quick decision to be made. He had been out with the other fighters and bombers from *Bunker Hill* attacking the Jap garrison on a small island to the north. A lucky shot from one of the few defending Jap Zeros—before it went down—clipped Scoot's oil line. There was a leak, though not a big one, and the engine was heating up badly. So Scoot had been separated from the others and now was limping home to his carrier, trying to get the best speed he could without overheating the engine too much. It had not been an easy job to nurse it along that way, for the oil was dripping away drop by drop. Still, he thought he might make it, for he had only about forty more miles to go.

"And now this clumsy boat of the Japs has to show up!" he shouted to himself angrily. "I could take him in a minute if I was okay, but with this leaky oil line—what'll I do? If I give her the gun and really swoop down on this bird, I'll force out most of the oil that I've got left, heat up the engine so much it'll burn out. But if I don't, then I'm just like a clay pigeon, sitting here waiting to be taken."

Scoot smiled. "Doesn't take long to make up your mind in a case like that. I'll get that baby who thinks I'm crippled and can't fight back. And then I'll just be setting myself down on the sea somewhere and hoping to be picked up, though there's not much hope for that here."

He let the Jap patrol plane come on, continued to act as if he couldn't maneuver the plane. He wiggled the wings as if he were trying to make his craft do something it wouldn't do. He succeeded in filling the Jap pilot with such confidence that the man was happily off guard.

Then, at the last minute, he gave his Hellcat the gun and she almost jumped out from under him. Up he rose, then did a wing-over and swooped down on the Jap plane from above and behind. Big splashes of oil were covering his windshield, forced from the leaky line by the sudden rush of power in the engine. The Jap plane was just a blur when Scoot pressed the gun button and heard the pounding of bullets from his machine guns.

Then he pulled up and to the right, looking out the side. Yes, he had done it. The Jap bomber was afire, but trying to turn to the left. Then Scoot saw what he was aiming for—a tiny reef with a few palm trees a few miles to the south. Suddenly the Jap plane blew up in the air with a roar. Scoot felt the shock of the blast and watched the pieces of flaming plane plummet to the sea below, where a steaming smoke arose from the water.

Scoot's smile was frozen by a hard hammering knock from his engine.

"That did it!" he exclaimed. "She's conking out, and right about now. Maybe I can make that little island even if the Jap couldn't."

He edged the plane around with the last gasps from the engine and put her into a glide toward the little spot of land. Then it occurred to him that there might be Japs on the island, tiny as it was, and with one hand he checked his service revolver to be sure that he might take a few with him before he went himself, if the worst should happen.

"And all that depends on whether I make it in this glide or not," Scoot said. "But it looks okay."

The plane was slipping down the sky fast, approaching the island. About ten feet above the water, Scoot leveled her off and pancaked into the water, trying to get his tail to act as a brake. The controls flew from his hands and his head hit the top of his cockpit. But he didn't lose consciousness from the blow, even though he was badly stunned.

He saw the rocky shore of the island rushing toward him as the plane seemed to skim over the water. Then he struck the rocks, was thrown forward, and heard a ripping, tearing sound as the bottom of his fuselage was crushed and mangled on the rocks.

He felt a throb in his forehead and realized that he was looking at the slightly twisted floor of his cockpit.

"Must have been knocked out for a minute," Scoot told himself.

He lifted his head and looked around. His plane was entirely on dry land. It had skidded over the rocks, leaving the water. Right in front of him was the smooth slanting trunk of a palm tree. He saw no movement anywhere.

"Well, if there were Japs here they'd have been on top of me long before this."

Scoot unfastened his safety belt and crawled from his seat, feeling his bruised arms and legs to make sure they were whole. In another moment he stood on the rocky shore surveying sadly his crumpled and twisted ship.

"My beautiful Hellcat!" he said, patting her side. "Look what I've done to you!"

Then he turned and looked the island over. It was, he could easily see, not more than two hundred yards long and fifty feet wide, and it curved in a gentle arc. There were rocks, a few palm trees, some low bushes and nothing else.

"Well, I might as well like it," Scoot said. "It may be my home for the duration!"

CHAPTER FIFTEEN

FIND THE CONVOY!

March and Larry stood over the navigation table and looked at charts.

"We're just about here now," March said, pointing to a spot not far east of the Philippines.

"What's that?" Larry asked, putting his finger tip on a tiny dot near by.

"A tiny atoll," March said. "Couple of hundred yards long, that's all."

"Let's pull into the lee of it and surface," Larry said. "There won't be any Japs on something that small. We can charge the batteries up full, get plenty of fresh air, and plan our campaign from here on in."

"Right," March agreed. "We'll reach it in about an hour. We've gone about two hours since the patrol plane left us."

So it was that Scoot Bailey, lying at the edge of the beach not far from his wrecked plane, which he had covered with boughs so it would not be seen by Jap patrols, heard a rushing of water a little way from shore and saw a huge black hull appear from the deep, not a hundred feet out!

He scrambled behind a bush quickly and peered out cautiously, though it was so dark that no one on the sub could possibly have seen him.

"A sub!" he exclaimed. "But the question is—Jap or American?"

He tried to find a marking that would tell him the answer to his question, but it was too dark to see anything. Then he made out figures of men on the bridge, two men looking around. One said something to the other, but so low that he could not make out the language. One of the men took up a lookout position.

"If it's a Jap," Scoot muttered to himself, "I'd hate to let it get away from me. I'm probably not in any danger. It must just be up to charge batteries. They wouldn't come ashore here for anything—nothing to come for, unless some of the men just want to plant their feet on solid ground for a change. Even then I can hide."

He thought hard. "Seems as if there ought to be something I could do, though one grounded flier against a sub is kind of tough odds."

He was so busy trying to think what he could do to sink a Jap submarine single-handed that he convinced himself that it *was* Japanese.

"The machine guns in my plane!" he exclaimed suddenly. "They probably still work if I can get at them. The plane's heading the wrong way or I could just shoot them as is. But maybe I can get one or two out."

Then he wondered if fifty-caliber machine-gun bullets could possibly sink a submarine.

"Probably not," he told himself. "But they could pick off quite a few officers and men. And then if the rest decided to come and get me, I'd get quite a few more on their way in."

Suddenly the Diesels on the submarine roared into life, and quickly settled down to a steady purr.

"Charging batteries is right," Scoot told himself. "That's just enough sound to keep them from hearing me try to get a gun out of my plane. Of course, they've probably got their own machine gun unlimbered up there. Usually do when they're surfaced like this. But—well, I'll see what I can do."

Scoot crawled over to his plane and started to work. Taking off the engine cowling seemed to him to make a terrific noise and he stopped to listen, wondering if he had been heard. The sound from the Diesels seemed very low. And then he heard something—something that made his heart leap.

"Car—reee me back to old Virginnneee!" sang a high tenor voice. The lookout was indulging in his favorite sport. Scoot leaped out on the shore.

"Yippeeee!" he shouted at the top of his lungs.

On the bridge of the submarine, March whirled around at the sound of the strange cry from the tiny island. Without a word one of the enlisted men had leaped to the machine gun and now he poured a round of shots at the shore. Then there was silence for a moment. From behind a palm tree came a voice.

"Say—have a heart!" Scoot cried. "I'm an American!"

"How do we know?" demanded March over the sound of the Diesels. He would like to have shut them off so he could hear better, but he wanted to keep them running for a quick getaway in case there was any sort of Jap force on that tiny atoll. The sound of the American voice sounded genuine, but you could never be sure. Too many Japs who had lived in America went back home to fight in Jap armies. They spoke English fairly well, some of them, and they had used it to trick trusting Americans too many times.

By this time Larry Gray had scrambled up on the bridge beside March who quickly explained what had happened. Stan and Mac joined them, wondering at the sound of machine-gun fire.

"I'm an American flier!" Scoot shouted back. "Crashed here this afternoon."

"Turn on the searchlight!" Larry ordered, and in a moment the powerful beam found the lone figure on the rocky beach.

"Only one man," March said. "And it sure looks like a Navy uniform, slightly mussed up. He must be okay, Skipper."

"Can't ever be sure," Larry said. "There may be a pack of Japs back behind those trees. It may be a swiped uniform, anyway."

"But he looks white and tall," March said.

"Yes, he does," Larry agreed. "But if he's an American—wait, he's calling."

"I know you can't take any chances on a trap," the voice came to them over the water. "You tell me what to do and I'll do it—to the letter."

"All right," Larry called back. "We're sure you must be American, all right, but we won't take a chance. Take your clothes off and swim out to us. We'll keep the light on you and you're covered at every minute with a machine gun."

On shore Scoot gulped at the idea of the machine gun pointing at him every minute. But he agreed, knowing that in a similar situation he would be just as cautious about any possible Jap trick. He quickly stripped to his underwear, leaving his clothes on the rocks at his feet. Then, arms in the air so the men on the sub would see that he carried nothing, he waded into the water, always in the bright spot of the searchlight. When the water came up to his chest he bent forward and started swimming, being careful to raise both arms well out of the water at each stroke. But he had to keep his head down and his eyes averted because of the bright glare of the light.

Soon his hand struck the steel side of the hull and helping arms reached down to pull him up on the deck. Two enlisted men and McFee were there, looking him over carefully.

"He's okay, Skipper!" Mac called up to the bridge. "Not a thing on him and he's as American as Uncle Sam." Then to Scoot, "How are you, fellow? Glad we found you. Come on up."

He led the dripping Scoot to the ladder leading up to the bridge. As he climbed over the edge, Scoot saw a familiar face—and almost fell over backward to the deck again!

"March!" he yelled at the top of his lungs.

"Scoot Bailey!" March cried, rushing forward. He threw his arms around the shivering and wet flier and pounded him on the back. "Scoot, my boy! It's really you! How on earth—"

But Scoot was shouting and talking, too, laughing and dazed by the many things that had happened to him in the last few hours.

McFee and the enlisted men looked on in amazement at the scene, but Larry Gray was smiling. He remembered the name of Scoot Bailey from the many things March had told him about his closest friend. And he had seen enough strange things happen in the war not to be too startled at anything that happened out in the middle of the ocean.

In a few minutes they had gone below and Scoot was wrapped in a blanket while two men put out in a collapsible boat to bring his clothes from the island. Scoot sat with the others in the tiny ready-room and drank a cup of hot coffee, while they talked and asked questions and answered them.

March Pounded Scoot on the Back

Soon everyone was brought up to date on the most important things that had been happening. McFee and Stan, who had joined them, knew who Scoot was and how he came to be there. Outside, word went scurrying around among the men that they'd picked up a Navy flier, that it had turned out to be the exec's oldest and best friend. Everybody felt happy.

"With a stroke of luck like that," Pete Kalinsky said, "maybe we can find that Jap convoy now."

March told Scoot about their search for the convoy, their encounter with the Jap patrol plane that very afternoon, and how the American plane had chased him away. Scoot was serious right away.

"Two-motored Aichi flying boat?" he asked.

"Yes, why?" March asked.

"I took care of him for you," Scoot said with a smile. "He *will* try to depth-charge my friend, will he? Well, he won't do *that* any more."

Scoot told them about his leaky oil line, his encounter with the Jap plane, shooting it down, and then making the tiny island in a glide.

"And then I came along and picked you up," March laughed, "with only a few hours' wait."

"Remember—a long time ago," Scoot said, "you told me you'd probably have to come along in your sub and save me from a bunch of Japs?"

"Sure I remember!" March cried. "Didn't know I was such a good prophet."

"You didn't save me from any Japs," Scoot snorted. "Just from boredom spending the rest of the war on that island. But let me tell you another thing—you don't know how close you came to getting killed."

"What do you mean?" Larry asked.

"I mean you ought to pin a medal on whoever it is in your crew that sings 'Carry me Back to old Virginny,'" Scoot said. "Up to that time I had decided you were Japs and I was getting a machine gun out of my plane."

"You mean you were going to attack us single-handed?" demanded Stan Bigelow.

"Sure—I didn't have anybody else to help me, so it had to be single-handed," Scoot said. "I didn't think I could sink the sub, but I thought I could wait till a lot of officers and men were on deck and pick off most of them."

"Now, that's the spirit I like," Larry said. "Glad to have you along on this trip with us."

"Oh—" Scoot looked startled. "I hadn't thought of that. I suppose I have to go along with you."

March laughed. "Of course, you do. We're not a bus service. We're out looking for a Jap convoy and we can't very well take time to run you back to your base or carrier before going on."

"Well, so I'm a submariner after all," Scoot said. "Nice looking boat, I must say. Can I look her over?"

"Sure, from stem to stern," Larry agreed. "But not until you've eaten something. I imagine that island didn't provide you with much of a dinner. The cook is fixing up something for you."

So Scoot got into his clothes and ate a delicious meal over which he exclaimed mightily.

"Say, there's something to pigboat service, anyway," he said. "I thought we ate pretty well on the *Bunker Hill* but this is fit for a king."

"Submarine men *are* kings," March said, and for once Scoot would not argue on their favorite subject of the past.

Soon they went to bed, except for those on watch, and at dawn the next morning proceeded on their way, submerged. Scoot was fascinated at the diving operation and looked with some awe on March as he carried out the complicated maneuver. It was only then that he learned that March had become second in command of *Kamongo*. March then led his friend on a tour of the submarine, explaining the workings of all the complicated machinery, introducing him to the crew, who welcomed him warmly.

"Not bad, not bad," Scoot said. "I begin to see why you like all this so much. Nice small crowd here, all getting along well together. And I don't mind the idea of being under water at all, the way I thought I would."

Scoot and March and Larry sat down in the wardroom to go over their plans.

"You see," Larry explained, "I have a hunch the Japs are following a course with this convoy entirely different from any they've followed before. They are aware that we know they'll reinforce Truk as fast as possible. So we're looking for them to take a direct route. But the Chinese reported that there was something strange about the route. What is it? It's that it is so indirect."

"Sounds reasonable," Scoot agreed.

"Well, they don't want to take forever getting there, however," Larry went on, "so they're not being too indirect. I wouldn't be a bit surprised if they went down the western side of the Philippines, as if heading for Indo-China or Burma or the Dutch East Indies. Then they might cut through east above Mindanao, the lower of the big islands in the Philippines. After that they'd make a fast dash straight east for Truk."

"Why wouldn't we catch them easily there?" March asked.

"We might," Larry explained. "But for some time they'd be under protection of land-based planes from the Philippines. Then, too, we'd be anxious to scout them out as early as possible, so our subs would be farther north, looking along the more direct routes. They'd have a chance of getting through without a scratch, but anyway they'd not have far to go after we *did* sight them."

"What do you want to do now?" Scoot asked.

"I'm heading west toward the Philippines trying to test my theory," Larry said. "But I can't make much speed, having to run submerged in the daytime. I'm afraid they may be out in the clear before I can get there, but I'm keeping my fingers crossed."

All day long they ran submerged, keeping a constant lookout. They saw a Jap patrol plane and dived out of sight before he got near them. But there was no sight of the convoy. Darkness began to creep over the ocean and they were getting ready to surface when Larry, at the periscope, saw a Jap seaplane.

"Over to the right," he said. "Doesn't see us. He's too low. We won't need to dive unless he pulls up higher again. No—he's coming down on the water. Must be something there."

March took a look and thought he saw a small island near the Jap plane.

"Getting too dark to see clearly," he said. "Shall we go over and have a look, Skipper?"

"Yes, let's do," Larry said. "I'm curious about a seaplane here. That's the kind that's got pontoons and is usually catapulted from a battleship or cruiser. You wouldn't expect them out here. They can't do long cruising."

March gave the order to change course, and they stayed under the water as they neared the island.

"Hope there's still enough light by the time we get close enough to have a good look," Larry said as he peered through the periscope. "Good thing it isn't overcast today or we couldn't see a thing. And I wouldn't want to hang around until morning just for a look at what might turn out to be nothing."

In another few minutes they were close enough to see, and Larry reported to the others that a small boat was just putting off from the seaplane which was anchored to a buoy in the little harbor. Scoot took a look.

"Boy, those periscopes are wonders," he exclaimed. "Sharp as can be. Sure, I know the ship. And there's two naval fliers in the dinghy with two Jap soldiers rowing them to shore. A whole flock of soldiers on shore. Wonder what it's all about."

As March and the others had a look, Larry told them all what he thought this latest event meant.

"Seaplanes come from battleships or cruisers usually," he said. "I think this plane might well be from some of the warships protecting the convoy headed for Truk. The Japs have got lookout posts on a lot of these little islands here—probably plenty more than usual right now. They aren't trusting to radio, even in code, any more than we are. And they're having a seaplane or two go out ahead of the convoy to pick up reports from their garrisons on the various islands. This is the plane's last stop for the night. In the morning he'll go back to his ship and make his report as to how many American patrol planes or subs have been seen in the area by these outposts."

The others thought this over and agreed that it was a likely hypothesis. Then Scoot asked for another look at the periscope, and the others sensed that there was some excitement in his attitude. When he turned away from the 'scope he said to Larry. "Can I talk to you about an idea I've got?"

"Sure, come into the wardroom," Larry said with an eager smile. "Come along, March."

They sat down around the little table.

"Now what is it?" Larry asked.

"Here's the idea," Scoot said. "I know that plane—all about it. They made us study those things, though I couldn't see the point of it at the time. It usually has two men in it. Two men went ashore. So the plane's unattended. I'm going to swipe it!"

"Swipe it!" Larry and March exclaimed together.

"Sure!" Scoot said. "If you can surface enough to let me out—later when it's good and dark—I'll swim to it, get in, cut the anchor, and be off before those Nips know what's going on."

"Then what will you do?" Larry demanded.

"I'm in a Jap seaplane," Scoot said. "Outposts won't pay any attention to me, because I'm right where a Jap seaplane ought to be flying along, going

- 118 -

back to its battleship in the morning. Nobody will question me by radio because they're keeping radio silence."

"All this is assuming that my hypothesis is correct," Larry said.

"I think it is," Scoot said. "At least it's what a hypothesis is—a good basis on which to work until it's disproved. So let's go ahead. You want to find this convoy faster than your sub can get you there. In that plane I can find it in a hurry—if it's there."

"You certainly can," Larry agreed, beginning to get excited about Scoot's idea. "But when you've found it—what then?"

"Well—I get word to you somehow," Scoot said. "Now, let's see—"

"I've got an idea," March said. "Scoot sights the convoy, gets a line on its size and direction, then turns around and heads right back again. He knows our exact course. He'll come down on that course at a spot we designate. We'll surface and pick him up there. That eliminates all radio communication—even if that Jap plane has a radio and Scoot can get it on our wave-length and use it. And if he did we'd have to be traveling on the surface to get his message any distance away, and we'd better not do that too much."

"Sounds okay," Larry said. "But what happens on that Jap convoy when they see their seaplane approach, look around, and then head back again? Won't they think that's mighty funny?"

"Sure they will," Scoot said. "And I can't quite guess what they'll do about it. Maybe nothing, just put it down as another Jap pilot gone wacky. Anyway, they won't feel there's any danger. But they might send another plane up to have a look and see what's wrong. I'd just hope to be on my way by that time and out of his reach. Anyway, that's one of the chances we take. While I'm flying there I can get the Jap radio in shape, so that I could radio a message to you if I saw I was going to be shot down. You could surface for a short while about the time that might be happening, so you'd get any message."

"Well," Larry said, "there are a lot of *if's* in this whole proposition, but for some reason I like it."

"What's the gamble?" Scoot demanded.

"You," Larry said. "Your life."

"And that's mighty little chance for the U.S. Navy to take if it means finding this convoy early enough to wipe it out before it reaches Truk. If the idea doesn't work, then we've just been wrong and missed our convoy. Maybe you pick me up safe and sound as planned and maybe not. That's all."

"What do you think, March?" Larry asked.

"Well—" March hesitated. "Well—I think it's worth a shot, if Scoot thinks he can get that plane away."

"That's the easiest part of it," Scoot said. "Remember what a good swimmer I am. I swam to get to the sub and now I'll swim away from it."

Larry Gray thought for a while before making up his mind. It was his responsibility, this decision, and he had to weigh it carefully. Finally he spoke.

"All right, we'll try it," he said, and Scoot allowed himself a mild whoop of pleasure. "Here's the plan, to get it clear. We surface in about six hours, when everybody except a sentry or two will be asleep. Scoot is ready to go and he swims to the plane. We stay up just long enough to see that he gets away, then we dive and set out on our course which Scoot knows. He flies toward the passage above Mindinao, where I think the convoy might be. If he doesn't sight it within two hours flying he turns around and flies back, landing on the sea at a spot agreed on in advance. If the weather's bad, that'll be tough, of course. We surface for a while, riding the vents and ready to crash-dive. So we can pick up Scoot if he's even near the designated spot."

Larry paused for a moment and the others remained silent.

"If Scoot sights the convoy, he can tell fast how many ships, what speed, what direction. He heads back for that spot on the ocean as planned and we pick him up. If the Japs send up a plane or planes to get him, and if they attack him, he'll try to parachute out with his life belt, or get his plane down whole or something so he can be picked up on our course. Anyway, if attacked, he may radio us about the convoy first if he's been able to get the plane's radio going."

"What do we do," March asked, "if Scoot does find the convoy?"

"Then we radio," Larry said. "The Japs may hear us, but we can't help that. But we'll go on in to the attack alone. We'll try to get under and come up in the middle of the convoy so as to scatter it in time for the other subs and the planes that will be coming after they get our radio message."

"All clear," March said. "Now let's set our course and select our spot for picking up Scoot."

CHAPTER SIXTEEN

DOWNED AT SEA!

"Not a sign of life there," Larry said as he looked through the periscope. "Beach fires all out. Down 'scope. Take her up."

They moved toward the ladder leading up to the conning tower, Larry first, Scoot immediately behind him, in trunks. He held a bundle in one hand.

"Hope I can keep these clothes a little dry," Scoot said. "I'd like to be dressed when I do this if I can."

Larry unfastened the hatch cover and hurried up on to the bridge. Scoot was behind him in a second, followed by March and two enlisted men who manned the machine guns at once. Everyone moved swiftly and noiselessly.

Scoot was already sliding down the ladder to the deck, with March right behind him. Larry stayed on the bridge, looking sharply toward shore at every minute.

"So long March," Scoot whispered as he slid into the water. "I'll be seeing you."

"Good luck, Scoot," March whispered back. And that was all. For just a second he watched Scoot strike out toward the plane, holding aloft his bundle of clothes and making no splashing sound. Then March turned and went back up the ladder to the bridge.

There he stood quietly beside Larry, who said nothing. March picked up Scoot's dim figure in the water, listening at the same time for the sound of an alarm on the beach in case a sentry saw the black hull of the submarine offshore.

"He's reached it," March whispered to Larry.

"Good."

"Must be unfastening the buoy now," March said. Again they waited in silence.

"Can't be sure, but I think he's climbing up on the pontoon," March said. "Yes—I can just barely make him out. Can't be seen from shore."

Then there was a long silence, tense, expectant. March tried to picture Scoot slipping into trousers and shirt, climbing into the plane's cockpit, feeling for the switches and controls in the dark. He'd probably have to wind up the starter. And suddenly at this moment, March wondered how much gas the Jap plane had in it.

"Must be enough for it to get back to its battleship," he told himself.

March jumped. A coughing roar split the silence and the darkness. Flashes of flame came from the exhaust pipes of the plane as the engine roared, subsided, roared again. Scoot had taken just half a minute to warm it up. Then he gave it the gun and March saw the plane begin to move.

"Down, men!" Larry shouted, and the two men left their guns and slid down the hatch. "Get on down, March," Larry said, "and take her down. I'm right behind you."

But at that moment shots rang out from the shore. Figures were running along the beach, shouting and gesticulating wildly. The seaplane was roaring away over the water and some men were firing at it.

March, his feet on the rungs of the ladder, looked up, startled. And then Larry fell at his feet.

"I'm hit, March," Larry said. "Don't waste a minute. I can get down. Hurry."

Grabbing his Skipper, March hauled him to the companionway. He heard the spatter of bullets against the sides of the submarine. He lowered Larry quickly down the hatch and men below grabbed him and helped him from the ladder. March slid down after him, shouting commands to take her down while he was still closing the hatch.

"Call Sallini," he said to one of the men. "Take the Skipper to his quarters. Mac, go in with him."

The roar of water into the ballast tanks flowed over them, and the whine of the electric motors told them the ship was under way.

"Steady at fifty," he said. "Hold course. We'll surface in a little while. Stan, will you take over here? I want to see how the Skipper is."

"Sure, March," Stan said. "Pat him on the back for me. Hope it's not bad."

March stood at the door of Gray's quarters. There was not room inside. Larry was on his bunk, looking up to smile with an effort, but with pain marking his face.

"This was one *if* we didn't think of, wasn't it, March?" he asked.

"How are you, Larry?" March asked.

"It hurts like the devil," the Skipper replied. "I think there's two or three slugs in my chest somewhere. Sallini will be able to tell in a minute."

The pharmacist was ripping off Gray's shirt and undershirt, which showed spreading stains of blood. McFee helped him, trying to move Gray as little as possible. Then Sallini examined the wounds carefully for a few moments.

"Three's right, Skipper," he said. "And they're still in you. I don't see how this one missed the heart but it must have or you wouldn't be talking now. This one up here busted your collar-bone. That's what hurts so much right now. And the other, on the right side must've gone right through the lung. I can't tell if any might be lodged in the spine or not. Doubt it or you'd have passed out—couldn't move much."

"Can't move much anyway," the Skipper replied weakly.

March saw that his face was draining white, and his eyes began to cloud over.

"Sulfa tablets, anyway," Sallini said. "And bandages to stop the bleeding here, though there's not much likely to come out while he's lying down. May be some internal bleeding but I couldn't do anything about that. Don't know what else I could do right now."

"Okay, Sallini," March said. "Go get what you need and do it as fast as you can."

The pharmacist left and March stepped close to the Skipper, leaning down close to him as Mac was.

"March," Gray said. "I don't know what the devil this is, but I feel like passing out. Anyway—and this is an order from your Captain—carry out plans exactly as we have laid them out. You're in command of this submarine when I'm—er, incapacitated. McFee will help you carry on. Go get that convoy!"

"We'll get it, Larry," March said. "But you'll do the job, because you'll be up and around by the time we get there. Or at least you can direct the battle from your bunk."

Gray smiled and let his head fall back. He seemed to be sleeping. Then Sallini reappeared and Mac and March stepped to the companionway and watched through the door while the pharmacist did what he could for Gray.

The Skipper was unconscious and they had done all they could. March, with a heavy heart, stepped back into the control room and took the interphone from the orderly.

"The Skipper's been wounded," he said to the entire ship. "I know that makes you all feel just as badly as I feel right now. Sallini's done all he can for him and he's resting. Can't tell much about his condition, but I'll let you know regularly how he is."

Then he gave the order to surface the boat and they went ahead on course in the darkness. March stood his watch on the bridge, looking ahead in the blackness, wondering how Scoot was making out up there, and how the Skipper was making out in his own blackness down below. Sallini had given Larry some blood plasma to overcome some of the loss of blood that the Skipper had suffered, but Gray was still unconscious. When March went below as Stan came to relieve him, he found Sallini worried.

"His fever's going up," he said. "I've just given him more sulfa. Don't know what it can be but there's infection somewhere. Wish I could get those slugs out of him, but that's a ticklish business."

"We'll wait and see," March said. "Maybe the sulfa will lick the infection and the fever will come down. If not—well, we'll decide then what to do. Meanwhile, get some sleep. You've been up all night."

March lay down on his bunk for a while and managed to drift off to sleep for three hours. Just as dawn was breaking he got up and had a cup of coffee, had the boat submerged to periscope depth, and traveled ahead more slowly, checking regularly to make sure he was exactly on the course he had agreed on with Scoot.

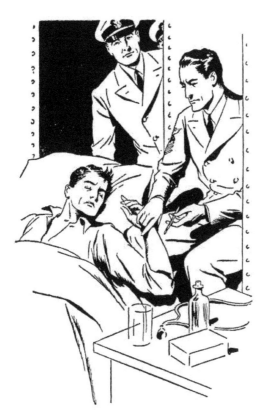

The Skipper Was Still Unconscious

"I wonder how Scoot's making out," he said. "He might be pretty near that convoy now—if there's a convoy there."

Scoot was at that moment disgusted. He had been able to do nothing with the Jap plane's radio during all these hours, and now, even with more light to see by, he could not get it working.

"Maybe when the Japs order radio silence," he told himself, "they enforce it by gumming up the radio some way so it *can't* be used. Anyway, I can't do anything with this baby. I'm going to be keeping radio silence whether I want to or not."

So he turned his attention to the sea ahead of him, where he hoped to sight the convoy. Looking at the chart occasionally and checking his speed, he calculated where he must be.

Then he saw it! First a few clouds of smoke far ahead on the horizon. Then little dots below the smoke—dots that were Jap ships. More and more and more of them he saw, line after line in orderly procession. Up ahead and at the sides were destroyers and near the front a battleship—no, two battleships. As he flew on further he made out a carrier in the center and at the end three cruisers and more destroyers kept a rear guard.

"Don't want to get any closer than I have to," Scoot spoke aloud to himself. "But I want to get all the dope I can and as accurately as possible. Got to stick around long enough to check their speed and course."

He flew on, counting, checking, making another estimate to compare with his first.

"About fifty-five ships," he said to himself. "Eight miles long, three miles wide. Pretty slow—there must be some old freighters in there. About ten knots."

He grabbed a chart and quickly plotted the convoy's course, wrote brief notations of his conclusions, tucked the paper into a waterproof pouch and stuck it in his pocket.

"Won't trust to memory, anyway," he said.

Then, feeling that he had learned all he could, he banked the plane and turned away, still about two miles ahead of the leading ships. He looked back down at them as he headed eastward once more.

"Right now they're wondering what's going on," he said to himself. "Up to now they haven't thought a thing. They saw the plane coming in and just thought it was a little earlier than they had expected. That maybe made them wonder if I had some special report. But now they really are in a dither! They just can't figure out why I should come so close and then turn back."

He laughed. "Well, that's their problem, not mine."

He gave the little plane all the speed he could. If they were going to send up a plane to have a look at him, he wanted to get as far away as possible. They might send up several planes.

"If they're fast, then I'm sunk," Scoot said. "But why should they send up a flock of planes to look at one Jap seaplane that acts a little funny?"

He checked his course often, so that he could land where the submarine could pick him up. And he kept looking behind for the Jap plane that might be coming after him.

He did not have to wait long for that. Half an hour away from the convoy he saw the fast little pursuit ship behind him, coming like the wind. He wished his own plane could travel twice as fast, but he could not urge another mile per hour from it. Gradually the gap closed between the two planes.

"Now what?" Scoot asked himself. "What should I do? I'll keep right on this course, first of all. And I'll just keep flying straight ahead as if I were minding my own business. Nothing much else I *can* do. That plane's got three times the speed and ten times the fire power of this one!"

The pursuit was only a few hundred yards behind. It stayed there for a while, apparently awaiting some kind of signal from the seaplane. Then it came around to one side, and Scoot tried to hide his face.

"First and only time I ever wished I looked like a Jap," Scoot said.

The fast plane flew alongside the other for a time, slowing down to keep pace with it, but still some distance to one side.

"What is this?" Scoot asked. "Are we just going out for a spin together? I wish he'd do something."

The Jap flier obliged by cutting back and coming up on the other side, then speeding up and circling around in front. It was at this moment that he looked full into Scoot's face. Scoot could even see the alarm that filled him, the wide eyes, the gasp of amazement, as he realized that an American was flying the Jap seaplane.

At that moment, Scoot pressed the trigger on his own machine gun, but it was too late. The Jap had darted out of range just in time. He was so fast that Scoot could not possibly maneuver his slow ship to battle him.

"There's only one chance," Scoot said to himself, "and I'm going to try it. If this monkey is the bad shot most of them are, he may miss on his first try, even with a set-up like me. If he does, that's my chance."

The fast pursuit was diving on the seaplane's tail. Scoot heard the staccato rattling of the ship's machine guns.

"Good!" he cried. "Firing while he's still too far away, like all of them! Too anxious!"

But then Scoot's plane wobbled, tipped over, and went spiraling down to the sea in a slow spin. The pursuit plane circled above and watched. About fifty feet above the water, the seaplane lurched a little, seemed to come out of its spin. The pursuit plane pilot looked puzzled, but he smiled again as he saw the plane stall, slip back and hit the sea, tail first.

CHAPTER SEVENTEEN

ATTACK!

It was the cold water that brought Scoot to his senses, cold water creeping up over his chest. When he felt it, he scrambled forward, but fell back in his seat at once. The arm he had reached out to pull himself up with would not work. It hung limp at his side. He glanced down and saw blood streaming from it.

"Got to do something about that!" he muttered dazedly. "Anyway, it worked. He thought he hit me. I did a nice slow spinning dive. He thought he'd got the pilot and the plane just went out of control, fell into a natural slow spin. And did I keep it slow! He must have thought it was funny when I pulled out of it just over the water, but I didn't make it look too good. Couldn't. But I'd slowed her down plenty, then put her into a stall and let her flop back tail first."

The water was creeping higher as Scoot sat there thinking of what had just happened. Then he shook himself to clear his head, reached up with his good arm and pulled himself forward. The door of the cockpit was already wrenched half off, so Scoot crawled out easily enough. But then he slipped and fell into the water.

The shock revived him a little more so that he grabbed one pontoon. Slowly and painfully he pulled himself up on it. Then he looked up into the sky. Far to the west he saw the dot that was the Jap pursuit ship heading back to its convoy. Scoot smiled weakly.

"He thinks he's killed an American flier," he mumbled. "He doesn't know how hard that is to do."

The plane was not sinking any further. Its tail and most of the fuselage were covered but the nose and wings and pontoons were above the surface.

"Only one pontoon busted," Scoot told himself. "The other's holding us up—that and the wing tanks that are almost empty."

Then he saw his broken arm again. He had to stop that flow of blood. He wriggled forward a little on the sloping pontoon so that he could wrap his legs around the brace leading from it to the plane's fuselage. Then he used his good left arm to rip off most of one side of his shirt. Holding one end of the strip in his teeth, he wound the cloth around the bad arm above the break, making it as tight as he could. It slipped a little as he tied it, but it was fairly tight. The flow of blood did not stop, but it was greatly reduced.

"Don't know how much longer I can keep my strength," he said to himself. "Better make myself fast somehow."

He Tied Himself to the Strut

Slowly he struggled out of his trousers, after taking the waterproof pouch with the convoy information and putting it in his money belt. Next he tied himself to the strut with the legs of his trousers. Then he sat, looking eastward in the direction from which *Kamongo* must come.

"I'm not quite as far as I ought to be," he thought, feeling consciousness leaving him. "They'll probably go right under me."

It was there that March found him. He had brought *Kamongo* to the surface a short distance before the spot agreed upon for the meeting. But there had been no sign of Scoot. Keeping steadily ahead on course, March had ordered all men to stay below at their stations except for himself and the controlman on the bridge. They were riding the vents, with main ballast tanks open, and air vents at the top closed. The water rushed in to fill part of the tanks, but not all of them, because of the air trapped inside. That still allowed *Kamongo* enough buoyancy to keep on the surface, but not at full speed. All that was needed for a dive was the opening of the air vents at the top of the ballast tanks. That might save twenty seconds in the diving operations and twenty seconds might make all the difference in the world.

March had looked frantically over the sea when they reached the designated spot. Still no sign of Scoot. And no report from the radio.

"Something happened!" he muttered to himself. "Something happened!"

So he continued on the surface—mile after mile beyond the assigned spot, in danger every minute from enemy planes that might sight him. Still no word over the radio.

He was just about to give up and order the ship to submerge when he saw the dot on the sea ahead. He was ready for a dive at any moment—but it might be Scoot instead of an enemy craft. So he stayed on the surface, and looked, looked, looked as they came nearer. Then he saw it was a plane, crashed in a crazy position. He ordered main ballasts pumped and full speed ahead. Next he ordered men up to man the guns in case this should prove some trick of the enemy's.

But long before they reached the plane they knew what it was. When they were still some distance away, they saw the figure on one of the pontoons. As they neared the plane, men were ready with a collapsible boat. Quickly they rowed to the plane, lifted Scoot into the rocking boat and took him back to the submarine. Lifting him up to the conning tower, they heard him mumble something. He reached the bridge just in time to have March lean close to his lips and hear, "Money belt—convoy."

In another minute Scoot was below in March's bunk and Sallini was hovering over him. And March was looking at the chart and the information about the big Jap convoy. He rushed to the interphone.

"We've found it!" he called to all hands. "Scoot Bailey found it. We're radioing headquarters, then going in to attack."

There was a whoop of joy throughout the ship. This was what they came out in pigboats for—to find a flock of Jap ships and send them to the bottom!

Quickly March gave details in code to Scotty at the radio and soon the message was flashing out over the water. In a moment there would be action on submarines, at airfields, in navy bases to the south and east where the Americans were waiting for just this news.

Then March took the ship down and they moved forward on a new course, planned to bring them to the convoy at the earliest possible moment. March figured it would take about two hours. By that time other ships and subs would be on their way, and planes would be roaring overhead soon after he reached the Jap ships.

He went in to Scoot and found Sallini smiling.

"He'll be fine," the pharmacist said. "Broken right arm, bad jagged cut severing the artery. But we've got the blood flow stopped now, got the wound clean and dressed. He's had some blood plasma and I'll keep giving him more as long as he needs it. He lost plenty of blood, but he'll be okay fast."

"Nothing besides the arm?" March asked.

"Just some cuts around the head and one leg," Sallini said. "Nothing serious. And exhaustion, too, but we can pull him out of that fast. He ought to be talking in a few hours and walking in a few days."

"How's the Skipper?" March asked.

"Still unconscious. Fever high but receding a little bit. Maybe he'll make it."

"Here I am going into battle with my Skipper and my best friend out cold!" March exclaimed.

"You've got the whole crew with you, sir," the pharmacist said. "Every man of 'em. Let's get in the middle of that bunch of Jap ships and blast the daylights out of 'em!"

Tension began to rise in the boat as they neared the convoy, traveling at a hundred and fifty feet where no shadow of a sub would be likely to be seen from the air. March got on the phone and told all hands the plan of attack, not minimizing the dangers.

"We're going into the middle," March said. "Alone. It was the Skipper's plan. We'll be the first there, and we're to scatter them so the planes will find easy pickings and the other subs can pick them off as they scamper away. We'll have all tubes ready to go at just about the same time—six fore and four aft. Then we'll duck for all we're worth and we'll go mighty deep and lay low."

There was another shout through the ship and the men stood eagerly at their posts. And then came waiting, tense waiting, as the ship moved forward. Men had a cup of coffee, smoked a cigarette, walked back and forth nervously. But they did little talking. They were waiting, listening.

Finally the sound man picked up something.

"Propellers," he said, "plenty of them—ten degrees to port."

"Take her to two hundred feet," March ordered, and then gave a slight change in course to the helmsman.

"We'll get right in their path and lay low without motors running. The sound detectors on the advance destroyers won't catch us, then. When they've passed over we can pick up motors again because their own propellers will kill all the sound ours make. We'll come up in about the middle, pick our spot and let go. I'll want the periscope up for just about five seconds."

The boat leveled off at two hundred and fifty feet. Motors were shut off. Soon the sound man reported the close approach of the propellers. March had judged right—they were passing overhead.

"Destroyer a little to starboard, passing over," the soundman reported.

"Another to port," he reported in a moment. Then, a little later, "Battleship."

"Boy, wouldn't it be nice to get that?" murmured one of the men.

"Nice, yes," March replied. "But that wouldn't do the job for the other boys that we're going to do. We'll let one of the Forts get that battleship. We'll just send it running."

The men nodded in agreement. They knew the Skipper's plan was best.

Ship after ship passed over as there was silence in the submarine. Then March spoke.

"Come up to seventy-five feet now. They can't hear."

The motors whined again and the sub tilted up slightly. Everyone watched the depth hand move to seventy-five and stay there. The sound man continued to report propellers overhead. March figured that they must be getting near the center of the convoy.

"Say, here's something!" the sound man exclaimed. There was complete silence as he listened more intently. "That's a carrier or I'm a monkey!"

"This is our spot!" March said quietly. Then he spoke over the phone to the entire ship. "We've found our spot. Right by a carrier."

There were a few cries of pleasure, but most of the men were too excited to shout. March gave the order to bring the boat up to periscope depth, standing by the shaft ready to grab it.

As the ship leveled off he cried, "Up 'scope" and the big shaft slid upward. March grabbed the handles and had his eyes in place in a fraction of a second. All the others watched him intently. He swung the 'scope a little to the left, then to the right. His voice came sharply then, giving the target setting for the forward tubes—all six of them. The men knew that was for the carrier.

Then March swung the 'scope clear around a hundred and eighty degrees and focused. "Troopship!" he called, and then gave the target setting to be relayed to the after torpedo room.

"Down 'scope!" he called. "Stand by to fire!"

The shaft slid down. Everyone in the boat knew that the periscope might have been seen even in those few seconds it was up, even though most lookouts on the convoy were keeping their eyes chiefly on the seas beyond the group of ships. The sound man would know if a destroyer came racing toward them. But March was not going to wait.

"Fire one!" McFee pressed the button that fired number one torpedo.

"Fire two!" The second one shot from the bow.

"Fire three! Fire four! Fire five! Fire six!"

In rapid order the commands came, then everyone waited tensely. March looked at his watch, counting off the seconds. Then it came—the roar, the shock of an explosion, and the mighty cheer that tore through the throats of every man on *Kamongo*. The first torpedo had struck home, but at that moment March called out, "Fire seven! Fire eight! Fire nine! Fire ten!" And during those commands the men heard further explosions from the first torps that had gone streaking out.

March had not been able to count how many had come, but he knew that McFee had done so. But now all were waiting for the first sounds from the aft tubes. In a moment it came—the first torpedo against the troopship, and March waited no longer.

"Take her down!" he cried. "Three hundred feet!"

CHAPTER EIGHTEEN

DEPTH CHARGES

Three hundred feet was just about the limit for them. Pressure was terrific at that level, they all knew. But they wanted to get as far away from the depth charges to come as they could.

Kamongo's motors whined at high pitch as they sent the boat angling down toward the bottom. As they went down March got the report that five torpedoes had hit the carrier and all four had ploughed into the troopship.

"It was hard to concentrate," said McFee, "but I know I'm right. And, brother, that's good shooting."

"Wish we could know just how much damage we did," March said.

"But you don't want to know badly enough to surface and find out, do you?" asked Mac with a grin. "The planes will find out when they come along in a few minutes. They'll tell us—later, just what we did. Anyway the sound man reports that the ships are scattering in so many directions he can't keep track of them."

Then March heard something else from the sound man. "Sounds as if there's solid rock below us—at about two hundred eighty feet."

"Wonderful!" cried March. "Settle down to it and we'll just lie there and rest. Shut off all motors. Then let them try to find us."

"Destroyers coming in up above, sir," the sound man said.

"Pretty slow, weren't they?" Mac commented.

March picked up the phone from the orderly and spoke to the ship. "They'll be coming any minute now. Hold fast. And we'll be snug on the bottom."

The first depth charge came far above them, and the shock from it was very slight. But then the submarine bumped slightly as its keel settled gently against the bottom. Motors were shut off and *Kamongo* tilted a little to one side as it lay down on the sloping shelf of rock at the bottom of the sea.

There came the metallic click and then the monstrous b-b-r-r-rroom of a depth charge to the right and above them. Then one to the left. Then one beyond the bow. Then one beyond the stern.

"Laying a nice pattern," McFee called, as he held fast to the little railing at the periscope well.

"That would get us if we were higher," March said. "They probably figured we're at about two hundred feet."

"They don't dare go any lower in their subs, usually," McFee said, as he braced himself for the next series of charges which shook him.

March looked around the control room. Everyone was holding fast, but looking very calm. He phoned forward to the torpedo room to ask how everything was up there.

"All fine, sir," reported Pete Kalinsky. "And nice shootin', sir."

Room after room reported everything all right. "Just a light filament busted from that last one in here," said the machinist's mate from the engine room.

March saw that one of the men at the controls was steadying another while he lighted a cigarette. He smiled, and then looked up sharply as a figure appeared in the door at the forward bulkhead. It was Scoot, hanging on groggily and looking angry.

"What's goin' on here, anyway?" he demanded loudly. "Can't a guy sleep in peace?"

March ran to him, but a depth charge—the closest yet—sent him sprawling to the floor. McFee picked him up, holding fast to the bulkhead while doing so. Then, between explosions, they got Scoot back to his bunk, where they strapped him in place. The young flier went to sleep again peacefully.

On the way back to the control room March and McFee stopped to look at the Skipper. Sallini was with him, and he smiled.

"Temperature went down—just about the time you hit that carrier, sir," he reported. "He's coming through all right, though they'll have to take those slugs out of him pretty soon."

Scoot Appeared in the Doorway

"We'll get him to a hospital," March said, and then grabbed the door hard as he heard the click and then the hardest explosion of all.

"They can't hear anything," he said to McFee. "Do you suppose they figure we're lying quiet down here and are going to send them deeper and deeper?"

"Might be," Mac said. March knew that if such were the case it would be better to try to zigzag away. The next explosion was so close that it knocked over two men in the control room who thought they were holding on fast. The next one knocked out the lights, and March shouted for the emergency system. In a moment there was light again but March was worried, trying to make up his mind what to do. Suddenly he felt that he just could not make any more decisions. He wasn't supposed to be a submarine Skipper yet, anyway. Why decide?

"Well," he said to himself, "if the next one's any closer I'll try moving away from here."

He waited tensely. The next explosion would decide the matter for him. He still waited. It didn't come. He looked at the sound man, puzzled.

"Destroyers moving away, sir," the sound man reported.

Then they heard another explosion. But this was different. It was near the surface, far away, and it was not like a depth charge. Then came another and another.

"What can that be?" March said, turning to Mac.

"Darned if I know," the veteran said.

And then it came to March. He knew. With a smile he picked up the phone and announced to everybody, "It's all over, folks. Those things you hear are bombs from airplanes—our airplanes chasing the destroyers away from us and blasting the daylights out of the convoy we've scattered."

The cheer that went up was tired but came from the heart. All over, men relaxed their grips, lit cigarettes, strolled for a cup of coffee.

"We'll just stay right here where it's safe for quite a while longer," March said. "Then we'll move on slowly—toward home."

Kamongo was limping when it came into port and tied up alongside the tender *David*. It had run submerged so long that its batteries were almost dead. But as they pulled into the little harbor the Skipper came to, first saying "Take her down! Take her down!" and then opening his eyes and looking around in a daze. He found plenty of story-tellers eager to tell him what he had slept through.

"It's just as well," he smiled weakly, when he had heard. "I never did like depth charge attacks."

Scoot was up and about now, his arm in a sling. He would not believe that he had complained about the noise that disturbed his sleep during the depth-charge attack.

No one was completely happy, though, until they had full reports of the convoy battle from the Intelligence Officer at the tender. It was with pride that March Anson carried the complete news to Skipper Larry Gray as he lay in the small sick bay aboard the tender.

"We got the troopship ourselves," March said. "The carrier was on fire and listing badly when the planes came and finished her off. Not a plane got off her. Of the rest, thirty-eight ships are at the bottom of the sea. Not one ship reached Truk!"

Larry looked at March silently and then a slow smile spread over his face. "Skipper," he said, "you did a swell job."

That was all the commendation March wanted or needed, though he wasn't dismayed later when he got the Navy Cross and his promotion to full lieutenant.

As for Scoot Bailey, he was flown to Australia to get over his broken arm before resuming his flying from *Bunker Hill*. The same award and promotion had come to him for his part in breaking up the Jap convoy, and he was very happy. But his last words to March were on the old argument between them.

"I won't say another word against pigboats," he said. "But I still want to get back to a plane. As I said once before, they make a great team, don't they?"

Lightning Source UK Ltd.
Milton Keynes UK
UKHW010745271222
414464UK00004B/308